D0328420

"Don't turn off the

Jack put the video camera aside. "Okay," he said. "For now." He stared at Paige for a long moment. "Close your eyes."

"What?"

"Trust me, remember? I'm the teacher, you're the student. Now close your eyes."

She drew in a shaky breath and fought to calm her beating heart. "I don't understand what this has to do with—"

"Sex appeal comes from the inside. You want to learn all about sex, then you need to realize your own sex appeal. You need to feel it, Paige. That's what it's all about. *Feeling,* not seeing or understanding. That's why I want you to close your eyes. So you're not distracted."

She drew in a deep breath and nodded. "Okay."

When her eyelids had fluttered closed, his voice suddenly seemed deeper, huskier. She could sense his nearness, feel the heat emanating from him. Suddenly, she was in a world where all that mattered was desire.

"That's it, Paige." He picked up the video camera again. "Now undress for me..."

Dear Reader,

I'm back again this month with another bad boy to heat up your nights! Jack Mission is a sexy, restless, love-'em-and-leave-'em type who returns home to Inspiration, Texas, for his brother's wedding. Temporarily, of course. No way is Jack trading his wandering ways to settle down. At least, that's his intention until prim-and-proper Paige Cassidy turns his world upside down.

It's bold, it's provocative, it's a BLAZE! I love writing for such an ultra-sexy line! And it looks like I'll be writing many more of these seriously sexy books. Look for my short story in the new BLAZE anthology, *Midnight Fantasies*, available in June 2001. And then watch for the launch of Harlequin's newest—and hottest—series, Harlequin Blaze, also in 2001.

I love to hear from my readers. Please drop me a line c/o Harlequin books, 225 Duncan Mill Road, Don Mills, Ontario, Canada M3B 3K9, or you can visit me online at www.kimberlyromance.com.

Enjoy, and have a deliciously sinful read!

Kimberly Raye

Books by Kimberly Raye

HARLEQUIN TEMPTATION
728—BREATHLESS
791—SHAMELESS

Don't miss any of our special offers. Write to us at the following address for information on our newest releases.

Harlequin Reader Service
U.S.: 3010 Walden Ave., P.O. Box 1325, Buffalo, NY 14269
Canadian: P.O. Box 609, Fort Erie, Ont. L2A 5X3

RESTLESS
Kimberly Raye

HARLEQUIN®

TORONTO • NEW YORK • LONDON
AMSTERDAM • PARIS • SYDNEY • HAMBURG
STOCKHOLM • ATHENS • TOKYO • MILAN • MADRID
PRAGUE • WARSAW • BUDAPEST • AUCKLAND

If you purchased this book without a cover you should be aware
that this book is stolen property. It was reported as "unsold and
destroyed" to the publisher, and neither the author nor the
publisher has received any payment for this "stripped book."

To Curt
I love you very much

ISBN 0-373-25907-7

RESTLESS

Copyright © 2000 by Kimberly Raye Rangel.

All rights reserved. Except for use in any review, the reproduction or
utilization of this work in whole or in part in any form by any electronic,
mechanical or other means, now known or hereafter invented, including
xerography, photocopying and recording, or in any information storage
or retrieval system, is forbidden without the written permission of the
publisher, Harlequin Enterprises Limited, 225 Duncan Mill Road,
Don Mills, Ontario, Canada M3B 3K9.

All characters in this book have no existence outside the imagination of
the author and have no relation whatsoever to anyone bearing the same
name or names. They are not even distantly inspired by any individual
known or unknown to the author, and all incidents are pure invention.

This edition published by arrangement with Harlequin Books S.A.

® and TM are trademarks of the publisher. Trademarks indicated with
® are registered in the United States Patent and Trademark Office, the
Canadian Trade Marks Office and in other countries.

Visit us at www.eHarlequin.com

Printed in U.S.A.

1

SOME MEN WERE JUST made for sex.

The thought struck Paige Cassidy the moment she spotted the man through the lens of her video camera at the crowded wedding reception.

It wasn't so much the way he looked, though he was handsome enough to make even devout manhater Imajean Strickner adjust her bifocals and smooth her heavy-duty girdle.

Tall and muscular and tanned, he stood just over six feet tall, his broad shoulders filling out the black tuxedo jacket to mouthwatering perfection. His ragged sun-streaked blonde hair caught the light and his strong jaw, sensuous lips and rugged air made her think of open prairie, wild horses and hot nights beneath a star-dusted sky.

But it was more than his appearance that screamed HOT STUD ALERT!

It was the way he moved.

She blinked and adjusted her focus, her gaze fixed on his lean tanned fingers stroking up and down the long neck of his beer bottle. Up and down, slow and steady, again and again in a sensuous stroke she could practically feel along her spine.

And the way he smiled.

She watched as he leaned toward the blonde, blue-eyed woman standing next to him at the bar. She whispered something in his ear. His lips tilted at the corners, lifting in an enticing, suggestive grin that made Paige's heart shift into overdrive.

And the way his liquid gray eyes seemed to deepen when his gaze snagged hers and—

He was looking at her.

Her hands went limp on the camera and she would have dropped it had she not been wearing the safety strap around her neck. He'd already turned back to the blonde, leaving Paige to wonder if she'd only imagined that brief, heart-stopping moment of eye contact. The intensity of his gaze, the heat...

"Say, there, Paige, how about cuttin' up the dance floor with me?"

The voice came from behind her and she turned to find Shelby Hoover standing there, his straw hat in hand. He stared at the worn tips of his Justin boots peeking from beneath the hem of a pair of starched Wrangler jeans and rubbed a hand over the top of his burred black hair. His black mustache twitched at the corners as he chewed his bottom lip and waited for her answer.

Unfortunately Shelby didn't rouse her hormones into an orgasmic frenzy, but the man did know his left foot from his right. What's more, he was ready to settle down. *And* he didn't go around flirting outrageously with pretty blondes.

Shelby wanted more. He wanted a house and kids and forever.

Just like Paige.

She glanced down at the bridal bouquet she'd caught and smiled. In Paige's mind, she and Shelby were a perfect match, even if he hadn't yet worked up his nerve to ask her out on a date. She wasn't giving up hope. Shelby was just quiet. Shy. Insecure.

Qualities Paige had known all too well. Up

until six months ago when she'd walked away from Cadillac, Texas, and a failed marriage. She'd headed straight for Inspiration and a brand-new improved life.

She'd been determined, but scared. Until she'd met Deb Strickland, the owner and editor of the town's only newspaper and now, the prettiest bride Paige had ever seen.

She shifted her attention to Deb who stood across the room beside her new husband. The woman had given her a job and some much-needed help, which was why Paige had been more than willing to use her newly learned video skills to record her friend's wedding to Jimmy Mission, the most handsome man in the county.

Unwillingly, Paige's attention shifted back to the bar. Better make that one of the most handsome men in the county. Jimmy definitely had some competition for the title since his younger brother had rolled back into town, and straight into Paige's line of vision.

She would have known Jack Mission anywhere. He was a legend in town. The cool, elusive drifter who wandered into Inspiration on occasion and then right back out. According to Deb, who knew everything about everyone in town thanks to her gossip columnist, Dolores Guiness, Jack was a legendary heartbreaker and *not* a man Paige should be wasting her thoughts on.

Her mind should be on Deb and making the best wedding she could. The woman had helped her so much. With Deb's encouragement, Paige had managed to trade her shyness for a little sass, her quiet demeanor for a more outspoken one, and her insecurity for some much needed self-confidence. Deb had been one of the few people to help her when her sorry ex-husband had walked out on her, leaving her the new girl in a small, close-knit town.

Woodrow. His name popped into her head and before she could stop herself, she lifted a self-conscious hand to check for any wayward strands of hair. Woodrow had always hated her flyaway mane. It had always been too long or too short. Too straight or too curly. Too... wrong.

Her gaze collided with a pair of liquid gray eyes and her hand stopped a heartbeat shy of making contact. Heat bolted through her, pushing aside a lifetime of insecurity, until she felt only the beat of her own pulse and a fierce expectancy in the pit of her stomach.

He was so handsome. Those eyes and those lips... slightly large for a man, but just right for kiss—

"Paige?" Shelby's voice drew her back around and heat rushed to her cheeks. She'd forgotten all about him! "Are you okay? You look a little flushed." He eyed her. "Maybe we should just forget the dancing and try it some other—"

"No," she blurted. Flushed or not, she wasn't about to discourage Shelby when he'd finally worked up his nerve to ask her to dance.

"Don't be silly." She put on her brightest smile. "I'm just tired of lugging around this video camera. I'd love to dance. It'll give me a chance to ditch this thing for a little while." She dropped the camera onto a nearby table and, with the bouquet clutched in one hand, took Shelby's with her other, determined to ignore the pull of the man who stood several feet away.

A few seconds later, she was moving across the dance floor as if she'd been born to it. Ironic considering she'd been the worst dancer in two counties up until a month ago when she'd enrolled in Earl Sharp's Dancing for Beginners.

Paige Cassidy had been the worst at everything.

It's all in the past.

She'd turned over a new leaf, started a new chapter of her life, and she wasn't looking back. She had been naive and clueless way back when, but she was changing things. She was rising above her background and bettering herself by taking several self-improvement classes.

The past was over and done with and Paige was looking toward the future.

Her gaze strayed of its own volition to the handsome man standing at the bar before she gave herself a great big mental kick in the butt.

Men like Mr. Made For Sex had only one thing on their minds when it came to women, and it wasn't the future. While he might be good for a wild, hot romp in bed, he wasn't a forever kind of guy, and that's the only kind Paige was interested in at this point. She'd fallen for his type before and found nothing but a world of heartache.

The next time she slid between the sheets, it

was going to be with someone who would be there the morning after and the morning after that. Someone who wouldn't take the best years of her life, then roll out of town one day with MaryJean Wallaby, the customer service clerk from the Piggly Wiggly with the biggest pair of boobs in the county.

Not a notorious love 'em and leave 'em type like Jack Mission.

No matter how her heart pounded every time she glanced his way.

AFTER THIRTY YEARS of living, there were only two things in life Jack made it a point *never* to do.

He didn't stand within stomping distance of a newly broken horse, even one that appeared as calm as the Gulf on a hot summer afternoon.

And he didn't dance.

Of course, it wasn't the dancing itself he had a problem with. That was the fun part. Bodies touching. Rubbing. Feeling.

His gaze went to the redhead two-stepping her way around the dance floor, a full arm's length of space between her and her partner, and he couldn't help but smile. The way he moved to a sultry George Strait tune involved two bodies getting to know each other, but not everyone seemed to have the same notion.

She danced the same way she did everything else—prim and proper. Like the way she'd held the video camera, her back stiff and straight, a serious look on her face as if she were filming a late breaking news story rather than a wedding reception. Or the way she'd held her back so stiff and straight when she'd caught the bridal bouquet. Or even the way she'd eaten her slice of wedding cake—her napkin on her lap, her mouth firmly closed after each mouthful, not a crumb falling on her cover-everything-up floral print dress.

His gaze roved from her shoulders down to her waist—where there would have been a waist if the dress had been a little more flattering. It wasn't. It hung like a sack, making her look shapeless from her shoulders to her trim ankles. His gaze snagged on the ankle bracelet glistening below her calf and his fingers itched to trace the path the gold followed.

Crazy. She wasn't his type. She was like all the other women here who'd practically fallen over each other to catch his new sister-in-law's bouquet. Marriage-minded. Every single one of them.

And dancing with such a woman, especially in a small town like Inspiration, was like courting. One led to two. Two to three. Next came dating and before he knew it, he'd find himself trussed up in another monkey suit, only he wouldn't be standing in as best man this time. He'd be taking the vows himself.

He'd made that mistake before. He'd never make it again.

"How about it?" An attractive blonde motioned to the dance floor. "You want to prove you know how to use those boots you're wearing?"

"I really appreciate the invite." He smiled and held up his bottle. "But I'm still nursing this beer, sugar." He touched the rim to his lips and downed a minimal swallow of the gold liquid.

"Later then?"

The refusal was there on the tip of his lips, but she looked so hopeful. Before he could stop himself, he nodded. "Later."

He watched as she walked back to the cluster

of women who hovered near the cake table, at least half of whom had already asked him to dance.

His gaze went to his beer. He had all of three swallows before *later* arrived and he had to make good on his word to all of them. Then again, if he took small sips, he could stretch it out to a good six or seven.

"Come on, stud. Let's dance."

"Sorry, darlin', but I'm still working on this—" The words died as Jack turned to find his new sister-in-law smiling up at him, looking every bit as beautiful in white as he'd imagined when he'd gotten word that Jimmy was finally tying the knot. She had long, dark hair, bright blue eyes and a figure that had undoubtedly lured his brother like a bee to honey. But Jack had no doubt it had been her intelligence and the sympathetic glimmer in her gaze that had caught ole Jimmy for good.

"It's a law," Deb told him. "You have to dance with the bride, particularly if the groom is busy talking new breeding techniques with his new stepdad at the bar."

Jack's gaze went to the trio standing a few feet

away—Jimmy, his mother and an older man with a gray handlebar mustache. The man slid his arm around Jack's mother and she smiled.

"She's had a permanent smile on her face since the two of them walked down the aisle a few months back. She looks happy, doesn't she?" Deb asked, her gaze following Jack's.

"Very." A welcome sight because the last time he'd seen his mother, she'd been dressed in black, a tear-dampened handkerchief clutched in her hand as she'd watched his father's casket lowered into the ground. A heart attack had taken the elder Mission several years ago while he'd been out riding fence. His mother had taken it hard, but just as his dad would have wanted, she'd eventually started to live again. He smiled. He couldn't think of anyone who deserved a little happiness after so much heartache. "Red seems like a good man."

"He is, and speaking of men, I've danced with everyone here with an X chromosome, except Jupiter Daniels, and word is down at the VFW that his X is questionable. That leaves my new brother-in-law."

"So I'm a last resort, am I?"

"Maybe I saved the best for last." She took the bottle from his hand and downed the last few swallows with one gulp. "Now you're all done. Let's go."

"Nice wedding," he murmured once they were moving around the dance floor. He caught the faint scent of apples and cinnamon and half-turned, only to see the redhead a few feet away, a serious expression on her face, her full lips moving as if she were counting each step. She was so stiff, he had the insane urge to haul her into his arms just to see if he could loosen her up.

It certainly had nothing to do with the fact that she had the fullest, softest looking lips he'd ever seen. And it certainly wasn't because he actually *wanted* to feel those lips against his own.

It was the principal of the thing. They were at a wedding. A happy occasion. She ought to be enjoying herself.

"That's Paige Cassidy."

"That's nice." He forced his attention back to Deb and away from the numerous ways he could loosen up the wholesome looking red-head. Ways that wouldn't leave her the least bit wholesome by the time he finished with her.

Even if the very last thing he needed was to touch or kiss or even think about a woman like Paige Cassidy.

No matter how much he suddenly wanted to do all three and a whole helluva lot more.

"She works at the newspaper for me."

"That's nice."

"She's pretty, isn't she?"

His gaze narrowed. "Get those notions right out of your head, little sister."

Deb shrugged. "What's wrong? You don't like girls?"

"Not that type of girl."

"And what type would that be?"

"The marrying kind."

"And what's wrong with the marrying kind?"

"Not a thing. They're just not my kind."

She gave him a knowing look. "You like those freedom-loving singles, huh?"

"They have their finer points."

"Yeah, they get hives just thinking about commitment."

He grinned. "Say, has Jimmy been giving you lessons on meddling? Because you're really good at it."

She gave him a pleased smile. "You think so?"

"You could have been born to it."

"Thanks, but flattery isn't going to shut me up." She eyed Paige. "Don't you think she's pretty?"

He shook his head. "I plead the fifth on that one."

"She *is* pretty. And she's smart. And as nice as they come. And I think those glasses make her look sort of sexy, in a Katie Couric sort of way. Don't you think?"

"You're not getting anything out of me."

"Come on, Jack."

"No way. If I agree with you, you'll haul me over there right now, and if I disagree, you'll probably stomp my foot."

"I'll do that anyway."

He grinned. "Either way, it spells trouble and I've already had more than my share."

She gave him an exasperated look. "You need to meet a nice woman." As if she'd just realized what she'd said, she shook her head. "God, what's happening to me? Freedom was my middle name. I've been married a measly five hours and already I'm the spokesperson for marital bliss." She shook her head. "You find your own woman. Just make sure she's nice."

"Yes, ma'am."

"And smart."

"Yes, boss."

"And pretty." He gave her a knowing look and she shook her head again. "Okay, okay. I'll stop. So how long is the prodigal brother sticking around for this time?"

He arched an eyebrow. "How long until you get back from your honeymoon?"

"Two weeks."

"Then I'd say about two weeks and an hour or so to pack."

"Smart-ass."

"I'm being truthful."

"I know. That's the problem. You don't have to run off the second we get off the plane. You *could* stick around for a little while." When he gave her a here-we-go-again look, she added, "This isn't about getting married, it's about settling down."

"If it looks like a duck and quacks like a duck, it's probably—"

"I'm serious," she cut in. "You can't keep

moving around from place to place forever. You're thirty years old."

"I like moving around from place to place, which is why I'm out of here when you guys come home. I've got a job lined up in Santa Fe next month with one of the biggest ranches in the southwest. They're breeding and breaking their own cutting horses, but their trainer's taking a leave for personal reasons. I'll be filling in."

"Temporarily."

"Yep."

"That's pretty far away."

"Yep."

She gave him a pointed stare. "Don't you miss your family?"

"'Course I do. But Jimmy's busy with you and his new construction business. You're busy with your newspaper. Mom leaves tomorrow to go on the road with Red for the senior rodeo finals in Vegas." Red Bailey was the oldest living bull rider and had nabbed the championship in his division for the past five years in a row. "I'd say my family's pretty much occupied for the time being, so no one's likely to worry about whether or not I'm hanging around. Say, I thought you wanted to dance?"

"We are dancing."

"We're talking. Now this," he twirled her and watched her smile, "is dancing."

The conversation ended, thankfully, and for the next thirty seconds they moved faster, spinning around the dance floor until the song played down and Deb gave him a hug.

"Thanks little brother and good luck."

"Shouldn't I be wishing you luck? You're the one who just married my pigheaded brother."

"True." A smile tugged at her lips as she stared past him. "But I'm not the one with a dozen or so single women headed straight for me." She gave him a quick peck on the cheek and murmured, "Be strong," before dashing off in a swirl of white.

Jack turned in time to see a cluster of women headed straight for him, each of them obviously ready to claim the next dance.

He glanced down at his empty hands and contemplated a mad rush for the bar. Then his gaze hooked on a familiar redhead exiting the dance floor barely an arm's length away.

She's not your type, cowboy.

Damn straight. She was like all the others, frilly and feminine and out to find herself a future husband.

With one exception. Unlike all the others, she wasn't headed his way. Why, she hadn't even smiled at him when he'd caught her eye from across the room.

For whatever reason, it seemed as if Paige Cassidy wasn't the least bit interested in him.

And it was a shame, a *damned* shame, for anybody to look so uptight on such a happy occasion. She needed to loosen up, and Jack needed an escape.

He took two steps and reached for her hand.

"W-HAT ARE YOU DOING?" Paige blurted when Jack Mission slid his arm around her waist and steered her back out onto the dance floor.

"Last I looked," he said as he swung her into his arms and started to move, "it was called dancing, sugar."

Paige fought to keep from stepping on his toes, her senses overloaded by so much male heat. He was too close and this was too sudden.

Just what the heck did he think he was doing? He hadn't even *asked* her to dance!

"I don't really think—"

"It ain't about thinking, sugar. It's about moving. You can move, can't you?"

The way he stared down at her, one blond eyebrow arched and a twinkle in his liquid gray eyes, stirred her indignation. "Of course I can." And she'd spent good money to make sure of it.

"Then prove it."

She had two choices. She could pull away, which wouldn't be easy because Jack Mission had a very strong grip on her waist, or she could calm down, concentrate and make it through the next few minutes without embarrassing herself. "What dance are we doing?"

"I'll let you pick."

"It doesn't work that way. Whichever dance we do is based on the speed and tempo of the song. This is a two-step. We should be going faster."

He tightened his arms and drew her even closer. "Feels plenty fast to me."

"It's too slow, and too close." She pushed against his chest and gained a few blessed inches of distance. There. Now she could breathe. More importantly, she could think. "We need speed and distance for this particular tempo."

"Feels like just the right amount of distance to me."

If only. Instead, Jack Mission filled her line of vision, surrounded her with his warmth and his scent and the hard, steady feel of his heart against hers—

The thought careened to a stop as she missed her step and stomped on the toe of his boot. Dread welled inside her. "Oh no."

"It's no big deal."

"I missed a step."

"I didn't even notice."

"I never miss a step."

"Never say never."

She glared at him. "You're throwing me off."

"Who? Me?" He grinned, a slow, heart-stopping expression that made her heart skip and her feet stall long enough for her to stomp on his foot again.

"Doggone it."

"Sugar, you need to relax."

"If you'll just tell me what dance you're doing, then I wouldn't be messing up."

"Are you always this uptight?"

"I'm not uptight. I just like to know what I'm doing."

"Darlin', just relax and breathe."

Breathe? Was he crazy? Dancing wasn't about breathing. It was about counting and watching your steps and...

Her thoughts trailed off as Jack pressed his hand into the small of her back and killed the few inches of distance she'd managed to gain. Soft curves met hard muscle and the air rushed from her lungs. Her nostrils flared and she drew in a deep breath. Bad move. His scent drifted across her senses, intoxicating her and she forgot all about trying to keep the rhythm and found herself taking another long breath. And then another.

He smelled of worn leather and virile male seasoned with a touch of danger that prickled Paige's nerve endings and sent a rush of excitement through her.

"That's better. You were way too stiff."

"I was in a classic dance form."

"It looked more like you had something stuck up your—"

"Good posture," she cut in. "That's lesson number one."

"Says who?"

"Earl Sharp at Earl's Dance Extravaganza. Lesson number two—" she said, trying to pull away again, but his hold was too strong. "There should always be a good six inches between you and your partner."

"That's no fun."

"But it's the correct way to do it."

"And not much fun. I like to have fun."

"And I like to know what I'm doing." Paige thrived on it. She never, ever wanted to feel out of control again, and Jack Mission definitely made her feel that way.

He winked and her heart fluttered. "You're doing just fine," he told her. "Maybe a little heavy on your feet, but I like the way you're stroking my shoulder."

Her fingers clenched as she became instantly aware of her hand moving back and forth across the soft tuxedo material covering his broad shoulder. His grin widened.

"So which rule talks about stroking, darlin'? Four or five? Or are you just improvising?"

"Yes. I mean, no. I didn't mean..." She frowned. Explanation? She had no explanation other than the fact that Jack Mission had made her forget six weeks worth of nightly dance lessons in less than two minutes. She'd stomped on his feet twice—better make that three times—and she'd forgotten everything she'd ever learned, especially the all-important fact that Jack wasn't her type.

Her traitorous nipples seemed to have an altogether different opinion.

As if he felt the throbbing tips press into his chest, he gave her a knowing smile and dipped his head, his lips brushing her earlobe. "You know, maybe you're not as uptight as you look."

"I am not uptight."

He eyed her for a long moment. "Darlin', you're as uptight as they get. An uppity up if I've ever seen one."

"I am not," she insisted, forcing her thoughts away from his delicious smell and the feel of his body against hers. She managed to concentrate for the next moment, until the song finished, and she finally, *finally* managed to pull away. She was about to turn and walk away, then her curiosity got the best of her. "So what's an uppity up?"

His grin was heartstopping. "Kiss me and maybe I'll tell you."

At his words, a rush of heat went through her and sent her pulse fluttering. For a brief moment, she imagined the press of his lips against her own, the whisper of his breath on her mouth, until her common sense intruded along with a healthy dose of righteous indignation. "*Kiss* you?" She shook her head. Was he serious? "For your information, I don't even like you." On that note, she turned to walk away.

His deep chuckle followed her. "Why do you think I asked you to dance?"

2

"HEY THERE, JACK. Jimmy and Deb leave you here to clean up all this by yourself?" Red Bailey clapped Jack on the back and twisted one end of his graying mustache as he waited for Jack's mother to finish saying goodbye to Judge Baines, the man who'd officiated at the wedding ceremony.

"They left me." Nell Ranger, the Mission housekeeper and the closest thing Jack had to family next to his mother and brother, rushed by carrying a box overflowing with trash. She wore a blue dress pinned with a crushed carnation corsage. "Those two young'uns have a lot more sense than to expect this boy to clean up after them. Why, he never picked up his underwear way back when and I'd give a pretty penny that things haven't changed much."

Jack feigned a look of outrage. "Get ready to

fork over the penny, darlin', 'cause I haven't left a pair of underwear lying around in years."

Nell stopped in the middle of gathering several dirty crystal plates and eyed him. "You mean to tell me you finally turned over a new leaf?"

"Not exactly." He gave her a wink as he shrugged off his jacket. "I stopped wearing the damned things."

"Just to get out of picking them up, I'm sure." Nell shook her head and proceeded loading her arms with dirty cake plates.

"If I didn't know better, I'd say you're blushing, Nell Ranger." Jack tugged his bow tie loose and stuffed it into his pocket.

"Nonsense." She deposited the plates on a nearby tray. "I gave up blushing the day I went to work for your momma. Why, if I had a nickel for every time you or your brother said something outlandish, I'd be a rich woman."

"Rich, huh?" He slid his arms around her bountiful waist and gave her a hug. "I've always wanted to find myself a sugar mama." He kissed her cheek before she shooed him.

"Just never you mind trying to help. I've got

Myrtle and the girls coming over to get this place in order just as soon as they take off their Sunday best."

"I'd be glad to help."

"And drive those old biddies to distraction with all those winks and smiles when I need to get some work done? No, thank you. You just take yourself off to bed right this very second. I declare, after roaring in here barely a half hour before the ceremony, you must be dead tired."

Amen. Which could explain why he'd done something so foolish as to challenge Paige Cassidy to kiss him. No matter how good she'd smelled.

His nostrils flared at the last thought. Her scent, all apples and cinnamon and warm woman, clung to him and he fought back a wave of need.

Yep, exhaustion made a man do foolish things, and Jack should know. After his wife had passed away, he'd spent the next six months barely eating or sleeping. He'd drank his way through those days, only to open his eyes one morning just outside of Vegas and find himself married for the second time to a woman he'd known for barely two hours.

Never again.

He was getting some shut-eye and forgetting all about Paige, how sweet she probably tasted and how he really, *really* wanted to find out first-hand.

At least for tonight.

Challenging Little Miss Uppity Up had been the most fun Jack had had in a helluva long time. Judging from the desire burning in her gaze for those few stunned moments before she'd summoned her anger, she was just as intrigued at the prospect of playing a little game of liplock with him. Just as turned on.

For the time being, of course. Paige had made it very clear that she didn't like him. That, alone, made her the perfect woman to help him sate the lust eating him up from the inside out. A lust she felt as intensely as he did. He'd been with enough women to make him somewhat of an expert and he could spot a hungry woman at twenty paces. Paige needed some relief as much as he did. Not to mention, she didn't have any romantic notions about him. He'd given up romance years ago when he'd watched the preacher throw the first handful of dirt onto his first wife's casket. His only wife.

I don't even like you.

Yep, she was perfect, all right, which meant that come tomorrow, Jack intended to pay her a visit and see what he could do to get Paige Cassidy to accept his challenge. Soon. Jack had never been long on patience.

He could only hope Paige was just as impatient. Otherwise, it was going to be a heck of a long stay in Inspiration.

"I HAVE TO HAVE THEM," Paige told the young man sitting at the desk opposite hers. "*Now.*"

He leaned back in his chair, his ankles crossed, his feet encased in a pair of orange flip-flops that matched the orange flowers in his Hawaiian print shorts. Wally, Deb's former copy boy, might have been laying out at the beach rather than sitting in the small office that housed Inspiration's only newspaper, the Inspiration In Touch.

Paige wiped the sweat from her forehead. It felt as hot as a day at the beach. Hotter thanks to the lack of windows and the lifeless air conditioner in the far corner.

"Would you just hold your horses?" Wally

took a long sip on the straw sticking out of his glass of iced tea before shifting his attention back to the magazine open on his lap. "What's the big hurry?"

"I've got an SAT meeting in a half hour and an hour's worth of work to do before then. I need to see the notes on your article so that I can write the copy before I go."

"Do it later. It's the beginning of the week. The issue doesn't go out until Friday."

"And I've got a week's worth of work budgeted until then. We'll never get the paper out on time if we leave everything until the last minute. There's work to do."

"You work. I'm on strike on the grounds of unbearable working conditions." Surprise lit his eyes as he glanced up at her. "Hey, did you know a woman gave birth to a fifty pound baby boy last week in Gentryville, Kentucky?"

"You actually believe what you read in those tabloids?"

"I do," said the fifty-ish woman sitting at a nearby desk. Dolores Guiness knew everything about everybody and was only too glad to spill every juicy detail each week in her Around the

Town section, also known as The Gossip Column. "Not everything, mind you. But those trashy things do print decent articles on occasion. Like that presidential wannabe and the floozy a few years back. Then there was all the hoopla about Michael Jackson and Lisa Marie Presley, some of which was garbage, but a lot of it panned out."

"But a fifty pound baby?" Paige looked at the woman in disbelief.

"It could happen. Myrtle Simpcox's niece over in Stafford knew this woman who had a neighbor who actually gave birth to twins that weighed twenty-five pounds each. Put 'em together and bam, you've got your fifty pound birth."

"See?" Wally shot her an I-told-you-so look.

"I still don't think it's a good idea to put too much faith in The Tattler. Now a real newspaper—" she tapped the copy on her desk. "That's a different story. Real papers report real news. They have a responsibility to readers." She eyed Wally. "Responsibility? Do you remember that concept?"

He gave her an exasperated look. "So what are you trying to say?"

"That you have a responsibility not only to our readers, but to Deb. She left you in charge because she trusted you."

"She left me to roast in this hell. I can't think in the heat. Give me air conditioning and I'm a super reporter. Until then, I'm struggling to keep my body temperature at a decent level. Want some raspberry tea? Jenny from the diner brought it over."

"She still have the hots for you?"

"Unfortunately." He shook his head. "By the way, you're making my life miserable."

Said misery had resulted from Deb's infamous column—Deb's Fun Fact for the Week—which Paige had inherited a few months ago when Deb had traded in her wild single woman status in favor of her upcoming marital bliss. The fun fact was a line or two of savvy love advice for the single women of Inspiration, such as "Sweeten Up Your Sweetie with Sweet Rolls" or "Light his Fire with Lingerie." Since Wally was one of the few bachelors in town, the single females of Inspiration had targeted him as the perfect candidate to test out the weekly fun fact. The tea was courtesy of last week's 'Tickle his Fancy with Iced Tea.'

"You should be thanking me."

"For robbing me of my privacy? For destroying my peace and quiet? For creating a town full of stalking sex-starved women?"

"On behalf of the women in town, I resent that. Privacy is overrated. Now hand over the notes."

"They're in the top drawer."

"The one right next to you?"

"Yep."

"The one barely six inches away from your right hand?"

"That's the one." He turned the magazine and studied the picture of the woman and her fifty pound bundle of joy from several angles. "True or not, this looks awful painful to me."

"I'll tell you what's painful," Dolores piped in from the corner, touching a hand to her gray coif. "I let Ida Louise over at the Cut-n-Curl frost my hair and I swear, she pulled out more than she colored."

"Well you wouldn't catch me letting Ida touch one hair on my head," Wally broke in. "The woman's as blind as a bat..."

The conversation continued and Paige let out an exasperated breath before stomping over to Wally's desk and hauling open his drawer. Retrieving the notes, she headed back to her own desk and sank down into the seat. Sweat slid down her temples, her neck, and she grabbed a napkin to blot the moisture.

Wally shot her a knowing look. "Told you it was better to keep still in this heat."

"Deb's going to kill you when she finds out you sat on your butt all week while the world passed us by."

"At the rate things are going, this heat's going to kill me a heck of a lot sooner than Deb will. Besides, she's a thousand miles away. How's she going to know if I took a siesta in the dying heat of the afternoon?"

"Because Little Brother's here watching you," Dolores said.

Paige blotted her forehead. "Don't you mean Big Brother?"

"She means Little Brother." Jack Mission's voice floated into the room and tickled the hair on the back of Paige's neck. She opened her eyes to see him standing in the doorway looking dark and delicious, leaning against the lemon yellow colored doorframe.

Wally's feet hit the floor. Papers rustled and his tea glass nearly toppled over. "I was, um, just doing a little research for a travel article."

"For a trip to Gentryville, Kentucky?"

"No. I mean, yes. I mean, I've always wanted to go to Kentucky. And speaking of going, I've got to do the 'This Is Your Neighbor Interview' with Loretta Marks. She's the new Sunday School teacher from Austin. Later."

"I wouldn't have thought he could move that fast considering the heat," Dolores said. She leaned back in her seat, aimed her handheld fan at her face and eyed Jack. "So what brings you here?"

"Returning my tux."

"Last I looked, Earline's place was up the street. You're at least a block out of the way."

"I needed some exercise. Say, Dolores, is that a new hairdo?"

Her curiosity faded into a sheepish expression. She touched a hand to her hair. "Why, yes. I mean, it's still the same style, but I had a new color job done just this past week."

"My compliments to your colorist." He tipped his hat and Dolores actually blushed.

Paige blinked just to make sure she was actually seeing correctly. Dolores Guiness never blushed. She made other people blush all the time with her know-it-all attitude and her all-seeing eyes, but never succumbed to turning red herself. Paige blinked a second time just for good measure. Sure enough, there was no mistaking the stain pinking Dolores' chubby cheeks.

"It's a shame you're out in all this heat, though."

"What?"

"I mean, a pretty hairdo like that won't stand up for long in this. Is it always this hot?"

"My, my." She clicked the button on her fan. "It *is* hot."

"What happened to bearable?" Paige arched an eyebrow.

"I can't very well go to the ladies' auxiliary tea with wilted hair, now can I?" Dolores gathered up her purse and her notes. "I'll just finish these notes up downstairs in the diner where it's cool."

"Sounds like a good idea." He winked and

Dolores blushed again before heading out the doorway.

"You're related, all right."

"What are you talking about?"

"The only other person who's ever made Dolores turn that shade of red would be your brother Jimmy."

"What can I say?" He shrugged. "It's a gift."

A few moments of silence ticked by before Paige finally found her voice. "So why are you here?"

"I was returning my tux."

"I mean *here*, here."

"You forgot this last night." He held up his hand and for the first time, she noted the battered bridal bouquet that he held.

"Thanks. I'd forgotten all about it."

"That's good to hear."

"What? That I'm having memory loss?"

He grinned. "That you were so shaken up after our dance that you couldn't think straight."

"You think so?"

"Darlin', I know so. You wanted to kiss me."

"You wanted me to kiss you. If I had wanted to kiss you, I would have." She glanced at her watch. "I have to get going. I've got an SAT meeting over at the activity center." She gathered up her purse and notebook.

"I'll show you the way."

"I know the way."

"Then you can show me the way. I don't think I've seen the new activity center. When was that built? Last year?"

"About five years ago."

"I don't get around town much when I'm home."

"Why are you doing this to me?"

"What?" he asked, as he followed her down the steps.

"Following me."

"Maybe I've always wanted to go to a SAT meeting."

"Do you even know what SAT stands for?" When he grinned, she shook her head, then elaborated. "It stands for Sick and Tired."

"That's just what I was going to say." He fell into step beside her. "Sick and tired of what?"

She smiled at him. Maybe it was a good thing he was following her. If he was so determined to make a nuisance of himself, the next half hour would undoubtedly change his mind. "You'll see."

"I don't know if I like the tone of your voice."

"Too late to chicken out now. Come on." She took his arm and tugged him down the street.

"SO I TOLD HIM," Harriet Miller said, "I would really like dessert." She shook her head. "Do you really need that dessert? Harvey asks me." She frowned. "So I said, I want that dessert. I deserve it, Harvey. I *deserve* it." Her words met with a round of applause from the other women seated around the circle of chairs that comprised Sick and Tired, the women's empowerment group Paige had been hosting for the past month.

"That's wonderful," Paige told the woman, desperately trying to ignore the man who leaned against the wall just inside the doorway, his arms folded as he watched her.

She'd expected him to run the other way the minute he discovered the nature of the group. Not many men felt comfortable in a group of venting women, but he'd simply smiled, said hello to several of the ladies he knew, and propped himself inside the doorway.

"So what did you have?" Louisa Jenkins asked. "The brownie or the apple pie?"

"The apple pie," Harriet declared with a smile. "With a double scoop of ice cream and caramel sauce."

"Atta girl!"

"You go, honey!"

"Score one for women everywhere."

"Thank you, Harriett," Paige told the woman, determined to ignore the way her skin flushed hot and cold every time she glanced at Jack. She was making it a point to avoid glancing at him or even thinking about him. She'd made it twenty-five minutes already. She could handle a few more. "That was a wonderful example of exercising your empowerment. Does anyone else have anything they would like to share? A moment when you realized you needed to speak up for yourself and did. Or maybe you simply realized it, but haven't yet had the courage to make the stand. Either way, we're here to listen." Paige glanced around the group, careful not to let her gaze linger too long on Jenny Turnover, the newest addition to Sick and Tired.

Most of the group was comprised of women

rebelling against their husbands, but Paige had the feeling that Jenny had more bothering her than a spouse nagging her to lose five pounds, or one that wanted his beer brought to him in a glass rather than a can. There was a glimmer of fear in Jenny's eyes that Paige recognized all too well.

"Anyone? Remember, we're here to help each other. To encourage and listen." The group remained silent and Paige clapped her hands. "Well, then, let's end today's session with a few words of encouragement. As women, we need to speak up for ourselves and do what we think is right. We don't have to fit into the mold that society has shaped for us. I hope you all remember that. And don't forget, you are special. You're entitled to the best things in life. Until next week, ladies."

After a little chitchat, the group disbursed and Paige turned to gather up her notes.

She paused, every nerve in her body going on instant alert when she felt Jack's hand on her arm. She turned toward him.

"Now I know what's wrong with you. This," he fluffed her ruffled sleeve, "is just a disguise. You're really a man-hater."

"I do not hate men. Just because I'm a capable woman and I encourage other women to be capable, doesn't mean I don't like the opposite sex."

"You don't like me." He seemed proud of the fact.

"I don't dislike you. You're just not my type."

"But you want me anyway."

"I *do* not."

"Oh really?" He fingered her nipple through the thin fabric of her dress.

She stepped back from his touch. "That's just physical."

"That's exactly what I'm talking about." And before she could say a word, his lips covered hers.

His mouth moved against hers, his tongue sweeping her bottom lip, begging her to open up and let him inside, and for a split second, she couldn't think or even breathe. Her heart all but stopped beating and she just stood there, feeling him against her, coaxing her, seducing her.

His arms pulled her close and his body pressed the length of hers, his heat overwhelming her until her knees actually went limp. His tongue teased and his lips nibbled and she couldn't stop her mouth from opening. He swept inside, tasting and stroking and stealing her common sense for a long, heart-pounding moment.

When he finally pulled away and stared down at her, she simply stared up at him.

"I was right."

"About what?" she said, still dazed.

"You wanted to kiss me."

"I…" The word *yes* was on the tip of her tongue, but it couldn't quite make it any further. "I'm late," she blurted. "I—I have to get back to the paper." She snatched up her purse and notebook and left as fast as her feet could carry her.

She needed to breathe, to think, to figure out what the heck had just happened.

It was the worst kiss of her life.

It HAD BEEN THE WORST KISS of Paige's entire life.

Not the kiss itself, mind you. That had been terrific. Wonderful. Stupendous. Jack Mission knew exactly how to slant his mouth just so and stroke his tongue along the length of hers and lick…

She fought down a sudden burst of heat that pebbled her nipples and made her walk faster toward the safe refuge of the newspaper office.

No, it wasn't the kiss itself that had been so horrible. It had been her reaction to it. The wonder she'd felt, the awe, the total cluelessness. Her mind had gone completely blank and she'd been dumbfounded as to what to do next. As if Jack Mission's kiss had been her first kiss ever.

Pathetic.

True, it was the first kiss she'd had in months, but it wasn't the first time she'd locked lips with a man. She knew how to kiss for pity's sake.

Okay, so she'd only kissed three men and one qualified more as a boy, but she'd had many kisses since her very first during a game of spin the bottle at a birthday party when she'd been thirteen. She'd been married, for crying out loud.

Can't you do anything right, woman?

The question echoed through her head and brought back a wave of anxiety. For so long, she hadn't been able to do anything right. She hadn't been able to dress appropriately or clean good enough or cook well enough or—

Water under the bridge.

She'd started a new life and broadened her horizons. Thanks to her weekly cooking lessons, she could actually do more than boil water. She could strip her no-wax floors better than Mr. Clean himself, and she actually wore more than just jeans and oversized T-shirts.

And the kissing?

Before she could dwell on the question, she heard a voice behind her. She slowed and turned in time to see Shelby gaining on her, his hat in hand.

"Hey, Shelby."

"I hope I'm not keeping you from something. You look like you're in an awful hurry, but I really wanted to talk to you about something."

"I was just headed back to finish up a story. You can walk with me."

"That's okay. I've got a load of hay to drive back to my place. This'll just take a second. Say, you did a good two-step the other night."

"What?"

"I saw you dancing with Jack. You did a good box waltz."

"That's what I was doing?" Of course it was. She would have known a box waltz anywhere.

Except with Jack Mission as her partner.

He'd pulled her close and she'd been conscious of only one thing—him.

"Look, I was thinking that maybe, if you're not busy next Friday night…"

Here it was. The moment she'd been waiting for. Shelby was actually going to ask her out.

"That is, I've been meaning to try this new steakhouse out on Route Five and I thought that if you like steak—"

"Geez, I'm late." She made a big pretense of glancing at her watch. "I've got an interview over at City Hall with the sheriff."

"Sure. I just thought that if you wanted to try—"

"Did you hear that?"

He glanced behind him. "What?"

"That noise. It sounded like Deb's cat. She's back at the newspaper office and she's been so lonely with Deb out of town, she's taken up howling."

"They've only been gone a couple of days."

"And the poor thing's already grieving. I really need to see about her and then get to my interview. I'll talk to you tomorrow." Before he could get in another word, she turned and started down the street.

What the heck had she just done?

She'd been waiting for him to ask her out. Hoping for it.

But that was before *the kiss*. Before she'd realized how totally inept she was when it came to interacting with the opposite sex on a romantic level. She didn't know how to kiss right! How could she go out with Shelby when a date was surely going to lead to an intimacy she was totally unprepared for.

For all her self-improvement, there was still one major hurdle she hadn't jumped. She needed some lessons in love. And she knew just the man to give them to her.

3

SINCE THE MOMENT Leslie Carter had asked him out to the eighth grade Sadie Hawkins dance, Jack Mission had been propositioned by many women. He'd heard everything from "I'd really like to get together with you," to "Take me to bed, Stud." But he'd never heard an invite phrased quite like this one.

"...to brush up on my technique and you seem like the adequate choice to give me some pointers," Paige Cassidy was saying, a serious expression in her warm chocolate brown eyes as she stared across the four feet of distance that separated them.

Jack set down the distributor he'd been oiling on his motorcycle and stood, wiping a trickle of sweat that slid from his left temple. "Let me get this straight. You want to sleep with me?"

She shook her head. "No, not at all. I intend to

be wide awake and paying full attention to everything you say."

"I meant *sleep* with me, darlin'. As in doing the dirty, the nasty, the bumpity-bump—"

"Yes," she cut in, a vivid red staining her cheeks. "I'm sorry. When you first said sleep, I thought you meant sleep, and I plan on paying attention to what you say."

"What I *say*?"

"And do. And don't worry. I'm a quick learner. You won't have to repeat yourself or do the same thing over and over."

"But that's half the fun," he teased, before he could think better of it. She wanted to *sleep* with him, for Chrissake.

"And I'll pay you. It's not like I'd expect you to do something like this for free."

"Pay me?"

"Twenty dollars an hour. That's what I paid Orlando Giovanni to teach me how to make antipasto. And ravioli, but that only took a half hour, so he only charged me fifteen." A doubtful look crossed her face. "But then this is probably a little more difficult than antipasto. I could go twenty-five."

"Twenty-five dollars an hour?"

"Twenty-six."

"Twenty-six?"

"All right. Twenty-seven, but that's my final—"

"I'm not bargaining," he cut in. "And I'm not doing this."

"Okay, twenty-eight—"

"No." He shook his head as the truth crystallized. "I should have known."

"Known what?"

He pinned her with a stare. "It was all just an act."

"What was an act?"

"You want me."

"I do not want you."

"You just offered me twenty-eight dollars an hour to have sex with you."

"You said you weren't bargaining, remember?"

"You do. You want me."

"I do not want you. I want to pick your brain."

"Darlin', it's not my brain you're asking to explore. It's my body and the answer is *no*." No matter how inviting the very vivid image was of her touching and tasting and exploring his suddenly flushed body. "You're not my type."

"And you're not mine, which is the beauty of this arrangement. We're all wrong for each other. I want love and marriage and a happily ever after." As if she noticed the sudden fear that rushed through him, she added, "But not with you. Never with someone like you."

"And what's wrong with me?"

"You're temporary, and I want permanent."

"Rumor has it you had permanent."

A guarded look slid over her features. "We all make mistakes and Woodrow was my biggest. But the next time, I'm not going to make any mistakes. So will you do it?"

"Have sex with you for money?"

"Do you have to keep saying that?"

"That's what you're asking."

"I'm asking for your instruction. You make it sound so tawdry."

"Darlin', this is as tawdry as it gets. You want to have no-strings-attached, paid-for-by-the-hour sex. That translates into tawdry."

"You're going to teach and I'm going to learn. It's no different from the dance lessons I've been taking. Or the cooking classes. Or the hair and make-up, the sewing, the macrame—"

"Macrame? You actually pay money to learn macrame?"

"I think we're getting off the subject."

"You brought it up."

"To illustrate a point. If I want to learn something, I have to find someone to teach me."

He eyed her. "You know what you're asking, don't you?"

"Of course. I want you to—"

Her voice drowned as his lips claimed hers in a hot, searing kiss that sent heat pulsing along his nerve endings. But it went beyond the physical, particularly when she shuddered in his arms and her lips trembled. A strange tenderness welled inside him and he had the insane urge to cradle her in his arms and kiss her harder, deeper, until she relaxed.

He pulled away and fought for a calm breath. He shook his head. "I'm only going to be here for a little while—"

"Which makes you all the more perfect. Here today, gone tomorrow. I don't have to worry about you getting any wrong ideas and hanging around like some lovesick stalker. Not that you would, of course. You're not really the lovesick type."

"I'm the hot sex type."

"That's what I'm counting on."

He shook his head again. "Sorry. You'll have to find someone else." He turned away before he did something really stupid, like kiss her again. That's what had gotten him into this mess in the first place. He'd kissed her and obviously wowed her so much that now she wanted to pay him for sex. *Pay* him, of all things. As if he would ever take money for something that brought him so much pleasure. He should be the one paying her—

Wait a second. No one was paying anyone because Jack wasn't doing this. He wasn't even *thinking* about doing this. He had a ranch to look after for two weeks, then his sentence was up. Jimmy would be home and Jack could get back to whatever waited for him.

The next town. The next job. The next woman.

For a little while. Then he was on the road again, moving, looking, drifting like he always did because Jack Mission didn't like to get too settled.

Settling was fine for some people, but he liked his freedom, his space. Yep, space was a good idea right now, particularly since Paige was filling up his senses with the warm delicious scent of spiced apples.

His nostrils flared and he swung his leg over the bike.

"I've got work to do."

"WORK TOTALLY SUCKS."

Paige spared a glance at the young man, his glasses perched low on his nose, seated at a nearby desk. At twenty-two, Wally was a senior journalism major at a nearby community college. As head reporter, he'd taken over Deb's editorial duties while she spent her honeymoon in Aruba. Paige had inherited Deb's actual assignments, including the Fun Girl Fact for the Week, which had become a major point of contention since Paige had ran an article about intellectual men. Since Wally was one of the few shy, quiet, brainy types in a small town full of ranchers, he'd taken Jimmy's position as the hottest catch for three counties. And he looked none too happy about it.

"It's not that bad," Paige consoled, despite her own trying day. She was tired and overwhelmed and embarrassed. Her thoughts went back to yesterday, to the shameless way she'd all but begged Jack Mission to take her to bed, and heat crept up her neck. "There are worst things than a few overzealous women."

"Overzealous?" Wally pinned her with a stare as he dangled a pair of fuzzy handcuffs from one finger. "Try psychotic."

"You're definitely overreacting. You should be thanking me for beefing up your social life."

"With a bunch of women who only want one thing."

"Hot sex?"

"Hot sex and marriage."

"That's two things."

"Marriage includes hot sex."

"Not necessarily." Paige knew that all too well. She and Woodrow had barely qualified as lukewarm on the rare occasions when they'd been intimate. Hot had never figured in except when it came to the weather.

She wiped a trickle of sweat near her temple and shot a glare at the air conditioner churning out hot air in the corner.

"Did you call a repairman?"

"I did better than that. I gave Deb a piece of my mind for leaving us here with the air conditioner from hell when she called last night for her daily nagging session."

"You didn't?" At Wally's nod, she shook her head. "She's on her honeymoon, for heaven's sake. Cut the woman some slack. She shouldn't be worrying over things like this."

"This is her newspaper and her two ace reporters are on the verge of heat stroke. You want to go two more weeks until she finishes sunbathing in Aruba for some relief?" A sheepish expression came over his face. "Besides, I wasn't going to bother her, but she asked. And then when I said not to worry, she badgered. And then she started threatening jobs. And with this being the only newspaper in town and me being desperate for credit in my senior on-the-job training, I came clean." He blew out an exasperated breath and tossed the box into his bottom drawer. "She said not to worry. She'll take care of it today."

"How's she supposed to do that when she's all the way in Aruba?"

"You know Deb. When she gets something in her brain, she doesn't let loose until she's done it. She thinks it's her fault we're in hell, so she's taking care of it. And all I have to say is, I hope she does it quickly, otherwise I'm liable to spontaneously combust." Wally got up and pulled his shirt away from his sweat-slickened back. "This is definitely the worst day of my life," he muttered as he headed down the back staircase.

Paige could sympathize. She wasn't exactly having a stellar time herself. It had started at 6 a.m., when half a cup of stale cappuccino had leaked onto her favorite white blouse while she'd been doing her best to get her old Plymouth started. Then she'd locked her keys in the car when she'd gotten out to walk, stained blouse and all, to Moby's service station over six blocks away. She'd hitched a ride with Sally Crumb and her triplets, and wound up at Moby's with a dozen grape jelly handprints to go with the cappuccino. Then she'd gotten a parking ticket for leaving the Plymouth outside of City Hall in a No Parking section. At lunch, the deli had put a half jar of mayonnaise on her turkey sandwich when she'd explicitly ordered mustard. And she was running short on money. And it was hot. And her hair was flat.

And it was her wedding anniversary.

Ex-anniversary, she reminded herself, blinking back a wave of tears. Not that she was crying over Woodrow and the fact that he was gone. That was the one good thing she had going right now. It was the principal of the thing. Today should have been one of her best days. In a perfect world, it would have been. She would have had her happily ever after. Her white knight. Her little house with a yard full of kids and a big dog named Shep.

Instead of marking another year invested in that happy ending, Paige was reminded of all the things that had gone wrong. Of all the things she'd done—

She forced the thought aside and busied herself pulling out the notes she'd taken while enduring the jelly covered hands of the Crumb triplets—she'd been stuck with Sally so she'd decided to profile the woman for this week's This Is Your Neighbor column. Might as well kill two armadillos with one slingshot, as her mama used to say.

"Today is what you make of it," she recited
Dr. Vaughn's power mantra. She'd read Dr.
Vaughn's book while she'd been holed up in bed
with a quart of chocolate fudge ice cream and a
box of chocolate covered cherries, mourning the
loss of Woodrow the Dud and feeling like a total
failure. That had been months ago, and since
then, she'd put Dr. Vaughn's advice into prac-
tice. She'd stopped taking responsibility for the
past and started planning for the future. "You
have control. You make your own destiny.
You—"

"I *hate* this damned machine!" Wally's voice
floated up the staircase. "This press sucks. My
life sucks. The Tom Triplets suck."

Wally definitely qualified as a major source of
negative energy.

"There are worse problems than having three
beautiful women hot for your body," she called
after him.

"True enough, Uppity. A fella could have just
one."

The deep voice slid over her nerve endings
like hot fudge over her favorite ice cream. A rip-
ple of pleasure went through her before she

could draw in a breath and fight for her composure.

A losing battle, of course, with Jack Mission standing in the doorway, a grin on his face. He wore a T-shirt and jeans and a grin that did funny things to her heartbeat.

"I'm not hot for your body," she managed to say.

"You're trying to get into my pants. That says hot to me."

"I didn't try to get into your pants." At his knowing look, she drew in another breath. "Okay, in a manner of speaking, I did. But you said no so that's the end of it." She busied herself arranging the notes she'd put in order a few seconds ago. "What are you doing here?"

He held up a tool box. "I'm here to fix the air conditioner. Deb called and said you guys needed a hand."

PAIGE CASSIDY WASN'T running after him. At least not in the traditional sense. And he wasn't putting too much money on the non-traditional sense either, not after four days and not one single contact attempt. Maybe he had read her wrong. Maybe she really didn't like him.

His gaze zeroed in on her luscious chest, on her nipples beaded beneath the stained blouse and heat bolted through him. Her head might not like him, but her body was sure tuned in.

The realization sent a surge of pleasure through him. Not that he was acting on the feeling, mind you. With her frilly dresses and her apple pie attitude, she was still bad news and he was steering clear of her. No matter how many hate looks she directed his way.

"...over there," she was saying.

"What?"

"The air conditioner." She pointed to the far corner and the lifeless unit before she directed her gaze at the pile on her desk.

Jack went to work, all the while conscious of Paige's every movement and the fact that she wasn't having a good day. Papers rustled. The phone rang an endless amount of times, but the kicker didn't come until she spilled a diet coke on her desk.

She cursed and her eyes filled with tears, and the sight twisted a knife in his gut. He had an uncontrollable urge to do something, anything to wipe the look from her eyes.

To see her smile.

Crazy, he knew, but he found himself blurting out the word anyway. The word he never thought he'd say when he first heard her outrageous proposal.

"Okay."

Jack had always been weak when it came to a crying woman. It certainly had nothing to do with the fact that it was *this* crying woman. He was a sucker for tears, that was all. Besides, she'd already proven she didn't *like* him. And he *was* attracted to her. What was the harm in acting on that attraction and enjoying himself while he was stuck here looking after things for Jimmy. "Okay," he said again, louder this time.

She glanced up with watery eyes. "Okay, what?"

"I'll do it."

Paige stared at Jack Mission, her Post-It notes quickly forgotten as she tuned into his words. He was looking at her with those liquid gray eyes and her body was tingling in response. "Do what?"

He couldn't mean... He wasn't saying... He...

His grin was slow and mesmerizing. His sensuous lips parted and a dimple cut into his left cheek. "*It*, darlin'." And then he turned and walked away.

And just like that, Paige Cassidy's worst day turned into one of the best of her life.

OKAY.

The word echoed through Jack's mind and followed him down the back staircase of the In Touch. He wasn't a man to entertain second thoughts, but damned if he wasn't having a few at the moment. Paige Cassidy was too sweet and naive and she looked much too good wearing a flower print sundress.

Christ, he hated flower prints. He liked subtle and sexy and he certainly didn't go ga-ga over a woman in glasses. But damned if he didn't like the way those too large spectacles perched on her delicate nose.

It was pure biology, of course. He'd spent the past six weeks training a bitch of a horse for a rancher in New Mexico. He'd been a hundred miles from the nearest town, and probably two hundred from the nearest woman. Then he'd gotten Jimmy's call with the news about the wedding and he'd headed straight home. He needed a woman in the worst way, and it was that need making him think all kinds of crazy thoughts, like the fact that Paige Cassidy actually looked sexy with an ink smudge on her chin.

Yep, he was suffering from deprivation, all right. And a mild case of stupidity.

"There you go thinkin' you can slip off without an old man taking notice." The deep, gravelly voice drew his attention and killed any more speculation on his sanity.

Thankfully.

The less Jack had to think about his fierce and immediate reaction to Paige Cassidy, the better. Thinking always got him into trouble and he'd had enough of that over the past years.

Jack turned toward the old man standing in front of the grocery store next door.

Twenty years had done little to change Cecil McGraw. With snow white hair and enough wrinkles to qualify him for some kind of world record, he still looked as ancient as the oak tree that sat near Jack's mother's front window. Time had weighed down on the man and his shoulders hunched just a fraction more than they had back when Jack had been boxing groceries for him after school. Otherwise, he was still smiling his lopsided grin, still standing out front with his white apron and his red bow tie as he polished the day's supply of fresh apples.

Jack smiled. "If memory serves, I only snuck away once and that was because you kept me here late working when you knew Janie Sue Grimes was waiting for me to take her to the movies."

"I was trying to preserve your innocence. That girl was too wild for her own good."

"You were trying to keep me away from Janie because your nephew had the hots for her." Jack shook the old man's hand and grinned. "So how are Janie and Monroe doing? What is it now? Thirteen years of marital bliss?"

"And two hellion boys to show for it. Mac and Mike are going on eight and twelve respectively, and about as much trouble as you and your brother were when you were their ages. They work for me on Saturdays, though they usually hinder more than they help." He shot Jack a knowing look. "Like two other boys I used to know."

"You still haven't forgiven me and Jimmy for stomping those five crates of grapes, have you?"

"Those grapes were for the ladie's auxiliary. They were putting up preserves and you boys ruined them."

"We were trying to make wine."

"You made a mess, is what you made."

"And you made us work overtime to pay you back."

"I'd have gladly paid for them myself and just told your folks instead."

"No, thanks. We liked the overtime better."

"That's true enough, otherwise your daddy would have tanned your hides and made you work the overtime too."

At the mention of his father, Jack felt a pang of regret. James Mission had died of a heart attack a few years ago while out riding herd at the Mission spread. Jimmy had been in Houston with his construction business while Jack had been running cattle out in Arizona. The news had brought Jimmy home permanently to take care of things, while Jack had stayed long enough for the funeral. Then he'd packed up and headed out the way he always did.

The way he always would because that was the way of things. Jack was too restless to stay still for any length of time and he liked it that way. He liked not knowing what each new day would bring. Liked seeing new places. He liked it a lot.

Too damned much.

He pushed away the thought and picked up an apple and took a bite. "I see you're still selling the best produce in the county."

"And I see you're still eating up all my profits."

Jack grinned and fished in his pocket for a quarter, but Cecil waved him off. "I got a better idea," the old man told him. "I've got two more crates just like this one out back. You help me haul 'em up here, and we'll call it even."

"You've got a deal." Several minutes later, Jack hefted the second crate next to the first two and dusted his hands off.

"So what brings you to town? I thought you were looking after the ranch for Jimmy?"

"For a little while. I'm doing a favor for Deb. The air conditioner at the newspaper office is messed up."

"T'ain't messed up, boy. It's got the devil in her."

He remembered Paige's comment about the air conditioner being possessed and he smiled. "Actually, it's got a knock I can't get rid of, but at least it's working right now." His gaze strayed to the second floor window where he could see Paige Cassidy's profile. She blew out an exasperated breath and her hair ruffled. "So what do you know about her?"

"Well, she's got about the biggest dadblamed mouth on a woman I ever had the misfortune to hear."

"Not Deb." He grinned. "I was talking about Paige Cassidy."

"Sweet little gal. A little shy."

Shy? Jack wondered what Cecil would think of sweet little Paige if he knew she was propositioning men for lust lessons.

Not just any man. You.

The knowledge sent a wave of heat through him that had nothing to do with the ninety plus September heat and everything to do with the woman whose scent still filled his nostrils. He inhaled and the faint smell of apples and cinnamon whispered through his senses.

"But then I cain't blame her none," Cecil was saying. "I'd be a mite quiet myself if I'd been through what she's been through."

"And what's that?"

"Got an ex-husband that's about as mean as a pit bull. She learned to tread softly early on and keep to herself, least that's what Myrtle Connelly over at the Piggly Wiggly says, and she ought to know."

Amen to that. There were two things that the good people of Inspiration could count on—winning the high school state football championship and Myrtle Connelly. She knew everything about everybody.

"Moved here to get away from him," Cecil went on. "He gave her an awful time. But now she's settled. Hey, know what else Myrtle has been saying?" Cecil asked him, a sly look in his eyes.

"I don't think I want to hear this."

"That you've been off in the big city stripping off your clothes for money."

"*What?*"

"Taking your clothes off, shaking your rump, doing the bump and grind—"

"I know what stripping is. Where would she get a ridiculous notion like that?"

"Beats me. All's I know is, Myrtle's got a twenty year accuracy streak and that's an awful good-looking motorcycle you rode into town on. Probably cost a pretty penny. Or maybe I should say, quite a few dollar bills."

"More like several broken bones. I trained a devil of a horse who kicked more than she listened." Jack took the last bite and pitched the apple core into a nearby trash bin. "Speaking of which, Jimmy's got a horse that's about to foal. I need to be getting back to work."

Cecil wagged his eyebrows. "Don't work too hard. You'll want to settle down someday and have a family, and all that shakin' and shimmyin' cain't be good for a man's equipment."

"You're funny. You ever think of doing stand-up instead of the grocery store thing?"

"As a matter of fact, you can catch me over at the lodge the third Saturday of every month. So why are you so interested in Paige? You thinkin' to court her?"

"Hardly." That was why accepting Paige's proposition was such a good idea. She didn't expect him to court her or get down on one knee. Paige wasn't looking for love or marriage or forever. Thankfully, because Jack had given up on those things a long time ago.

But right now… He believed in *now*, in living for the moment and making every second count.

Starting tonight.

4

"YOU'RE HERE," Paige blurted the second she opened the door to find Jack Mission standing on her doorstep.

It wasn't so much the fact that he was standing right in front of her, looking so tall and good-looking in a black Harley T-shirt and matching jeans. It was the fact that he was standing right in front of her, looking so tall and good-looking, while she looked nothing short of frightening in an oversized T-shirt and faded exercise shorts, her hair a damp, lifeless mess. "You're not supposed to be here."

His grin was slow and intoxicating. "True enough," he drawled in a deep, rich voice that melted her faster than her favorite caramel sauce melted a double scoop of Oreo Cookie Dough ice cream. "I'm supposed to be there." He motioned past her toward the living room and winked. "I will be just as soon as you invite me in."

The comment brought to mind a dozen or so images that had haunted her ever since he'd given her his decision. Visions of Jack, dark and naked against her daisy print sheets. Jack poised over her. Jack grinning down at her. Jack kissing her. Jack touching her... *Jack.*

"Sugar? You all right?"

"Yes. I mean, no. I mean..." She swallowed and shifted behind the door, away from his eyes—grayer than gray eyes that looked her up and down and every spot in between. "I wasn't expecting you."

"I said I'd do it this afternoon."

"But you didn't say when you'd do it."

"I'm saying now." He gave her another slow, wicked grin. *"Now."*

The word sent a spurt of anxiety through her and her breath caught. As much as she wanted this, dreamt of it the past few days since Jack had roared back into town on his motorcycle, the reality was a lot more intimidating.

"You can't just show up out of the blue. There are rules." At his puzzled stare, she added, "There are supposed to be rules. Every class I've ever taken had rules. For instance, the class always meets at a certain hour, for a certain length of time. There's usually a course syllabus that touches on what each lesson will cover. Then there is the required reading." At his pointed stare, she rushed on, "Not that we could really find a book for this. I mean, we could, but I'd probably have to drive in to Austin to one of those big book stores that has a special interest sec—"

"You're nervous," he cut in, a knowing light in his liquid gray eyes.

"I am not." What was she saying? She *was* nervous. But it was one thing for her to know it, and quite another for Jack Mission to be aware of her frazzled state. But he was. He stared at her with those observant eyes and saw everything she wanted to conceal. Her insecurity, her anxiety, her fear...

No fear.

She'd promised herself to put aside her fears a long time ago. So what if Jack saw all those things? She wasn't up for the Sex Kitten of the Year award, as he was well aware. No self-respecting sex kitten would need to proposition a man for lessons.

And that's exactly what Paige had done, a telling act in regard to her lust life, or lack of. So it didn't matter if Jack saw her hands tremble, or if he reached out and enfolded her fingers, cradling them against his warm palms for a long moment that actually sent a rush of calm, soothing warmth through her. It didn't matter because she wasn't trying to hide anything.

"We don't have to do this," he told her, his voice as soothing as his touch.

"We do. I do." She shook her head. "I want this." Because she was tired of being a failure, tired of feeling second best, tired of fighting the words that Woodrow had preached for so long—*you're not good enough.* Once upon a time that might have been true, but no more. She was changing, growing, evolving, and never again would she let anyone make her feel inferior. "I need this."

He didn't say anything. He simply stared at her with those see-everything eyes as if looking for something. "You're sure?" When she nodded, he gave her a sexy grin and reached for her hand. "Then let's get start—"

"But not now," she cut in, suddenly conscious

of the glide of sweat near her temple, the way her perspiration-dampened shirt clung to her. She looked a mess. Worse, she smelled like one.

"I've been busy with the shelter garage sale all day."

"Looks like you're done now."

"You don't understand. The garage sale was at Clara Petrie's house."

"And?"

"Clara Petrie, as in the Petrie Pack."

"What's the Petrie Pack?"

"The fifteen psycho mutts she adopted from the homeless animal shelter over in Grant County. They're very affectionate."

He wrinkled his nose and leaned in, taking a whiff of her. "Obviously. So how many did you get stuck petting?"

"All fifteen and one even sat on my lap while I rang up customers. I've never been licked so much in my entire life."

"We'll have to change that."

The words slid into her ears, so rich and suggestive and a burst of heat shot through her, making her forget for the space of two heartbeats, that she was hot and smelly and hardly up for a night of hot sex.

Sanity returned when she caught a glimpse of her reflection in a nearby mirror. One word...scary.

"Tonight really isn't a good night."

"The garage sale is over, right?"

"Yes, but I still have a ton of things to do. With Deb out, Wally and I are working overtime. Not to mention, Cindy's waiting."

He arched one eyebrow at her. "Cindy?"

"I watch either Cindy or Naomi for an hour every day after work." She motioned to the television behind her where a buff Cindy Crawford did stomach crunches. Her gaze drank in the woman's perfect face and body. *If only.*

She forced aside the thought. A girl worked with what she had, and while Playboy wasn't about to come knocking on her door any time soon, she wasn't a total loser. She was plain, a little too small in the chest and a little too big in the hips, but she did have nice hair and eyes.

Hair and eyes, she told herself, focusing on the positive. It was all about focus, about ignoring her doubts, being proud of her attributes and correcting her deficits.

Unfortunately, her hips topped the deficit list and her thighs ran a close second.

"I can't miss my exercise video." She drew in a deep breath and wished she hadn't. His gaze riveted on her chest and the way her nipples pressed against her T-shirt. "It's good for the heart," she rushed on, eager to ignore the answering tingle that rippled through her. "It gets the blood pumping."

"Amen to that, darlin'. My blood is definitely pumping."

"Not yours. Mine." She glanced at her watch and tried to force her nervousness aside. "Which is why I really should get back on schedule. I still have to prepare for tomorrow's cooking lesson, then there's the bird to feed and my kitchen to clean and I've got to work on an article for the newspaper and—"

"You're not a very spontaneous person, are you?" he cut in.

"I'm just busy. That's why I write everything down. Otherwise, I'd forget something." And she couldn't do that. She was on her way up and she wasn't about to get sidetracked just because she was every bit as forgetful as Woodrow had always said.

Damn woman. You'd forget you're ever-lovin' head if it wasn't attached.

No more, she told herself for the umpteenth time. She might not have a crackerjack memory, but that was okay. A person just compensated for their shortcomings and all was right with the world.

She turned and walked to the coffee table, grateful for a few moments of distance and some Jack-free air. He smelled too good, felt too warm and when he smiled…

Her heart double-thumped and her fingers fumbled for the day planner.

"Let's see," she said, opening the book. "I've got cooking class on Tuesdays and Thursday evenings."

"Right before the exercise video, I see." The deep voice came from behind her. She half-turned to find him looking over her shoulder, so close his scent wafted through her nostrils and his heat reached out to her. "So what are you cooking tomorrow?"

"Beignets. They're French donuts fried and dipped in powdered sugar."

"Sounds sweet."

"They are."

"You are," he said leaning forward until his

breath brushed her lips. "I can still taste you, Paige. I lick my lips and you're there."

"I..." Unconsciously, she licked her own lips and remembered the sweetness of his mouth on hers, the way he'd ate at her, stroked her, devoured her.

"So, are you going to give me a taste?"

"I haven't even made the dough yet."

"Not the donuts. You, darlin'. *You.*"

His eyes were mesmerizing, pulling her in, making her forget everything except the sudden heat that pulsed through her body. Her lips trembled, her hands shook and—

Slapppppp. The appointment book sailed to the floor, the sound jerking her back to reality, to her video which played in the background without her.

She snatched up the book and flipped to the right page. "I've got canning and preserving on Monday, Wednesday and Fridays," she blurted. "Then I do a yoga class after that."

"You have a wide variety of interests."

"I'm well-rounded."

"In all the right places." The comment drew her gaze and despite the way her heart thundered, she couldn't help but return his smile. He was every bit as charming as his brother, but with an edge than hinted at something deeper inside him. An intensity that made her heart pump even more than when he smiled.

"I finish up yoga pretty early. We could do it after that."

"On Monday, Wednesdays and Fridays?" At her nod, he grinned. "I suppose that could work, but I'm warning you, there might be a lot of homework involved. I'm a stickler when it comes to perfection. If we don't get it right the first time, we have to keep trying. And trying."

"Homework…" The question trailed off as heat rushed to her cheeks and she noted his grin. "Oh." She diverted her gaze and fixed it on the open planner in her hands. "How about eight?"

"Eight," he agreed, closing the door behind him. Suddenly her living room seemed a lot smaller than it ever had before.

"It's not eight," she pointed out as he stepped toward her.

"Not yet."

"But it's not Monday, Wednesday or Friday." Another two steps and he reached her.

"Not yet."

"And you're not leaving."

"Doesn't look like I am. I'm still waiting for a taste." Before she had a chance to breathe, much less think of a comeback, he dipped his head and his lips covered hers.

The kiss started out fierce, his lips hot and wet and intense. His tongue pushed deep and he devoured her, licking and tasting and stealing her breath. Her thoughts scattered, her body trembled and she whimpered, overwhelmed by the sheer intensity of this hot, hard, *hungry* man.

But the moment he heard the sound, the situation changed. His lips softened and slanted. Where he'd set the pace before, he pulled back just enough to let her join in. And then Paige did what she'd been wanting to do since the first moment she'd set eyes on Jack Mission—she kissed him back.

She took things slow at first. Tentative. She slid her tongue into his mouth, explored the interior and drank in his sweet breath, and this time, it was Jack who made the noise. He growled, long and low and deep, and a sense of empowerment rushed through Paige. For a few moments, she could actually believe he was as turned on by the kiss as she was.

Until he pulled away.

"Tomorrow," he whispered and before she could open her eyes, she heard the door slam shut.

By the time she managed to get her shaky legs to move, the sound of a motorcycle vibrated in the air. She reached the front window just in time to see his taillight as he whisked off into the night, leaving her alone.

The thought should have sent a rush of relief through her. After all, she was a smelly mess, not to mention she hadn't allowed time for any lessons tonight. She had a million things to do and she was already dead tired. Yes, she should have felt relieved.

She did.

At least that's what she told herself as she stood watching his taillight fade and listening to the pounding of her own frantic heart. The trouble was, it sure *felt* like loneliness. A feeling Paige knew all too well.

One she had no intention of getting cozy with *ever* again.

When she gave her heart to a man, it would be to the right one. Someone who wanted a house and kids and forever.

A man completely opposite to restless wanderer Jack Mission.

WHAT IN THE NAME OF SWEET sanity had he done?

The question echoed through Jack's mind as he revved the engine and sent the bike screaming down the highway, headed toward the Mission Ranch.

He'd meant to kiss her fast and furious, to drink in the taste of her the way he chugged a bottle of tequila when he was of a mind to forget the world and everything in it, with no thought to the hows or whys, just the outcome—pure, fuzzy-headed bliss. That's how sex was for him. An escape. A pleasurable one, of course, but an escape nonetheless.

But there was something about Paige Cassidy that made him want to pull back, to take things slow and easy, to savor the moment and think about everything along the way—how her fingertips felt gliding over his skin, how her tongue swept his bottom lip, how her breasts quivered when her nipples grazed his chest…

Christ, it really was too damned hot here. Otherwise, he wouldn't be having such foolish thoughts. Hell, he never should have *done* such a foolish thing as to slow his pace in the first place.

But he couldn't help himself. He hadn't had a woman in months. He'd come off the job in New Mexico and straight here with no stops in between. He wasn't used to going long without a little female company, so it was understandable he would want to really enjoy himself, to live and breathe every moment when coming off such a long, barren stretch.

Jack preferred that explanation to the other side of the coin—the fact that she smelled and spoke and looked sweeter than any woman he'd ever cozied up with. He didn't go for sweet. He liked his women a bit more worldly, uninhibited, wild. A woman not afraid to name her poison or her position and have a little fun.

That's what it was all about. Having fun. Living for the moment. Taking what he could get right now because tomorrow didn't offer any guarantees. He'd found that out for himself when he'd lost his first wife.

One day he'd been planning his future, and the next he'd watched his dreams lowered into the ground.

He wasn't going down that path again, which was why he'd stuck to temporary women.

Paige Cassidy, with her dreams of a happily ever after, hardly qualified.

But then he'd always been a man of his word, and he *had* agreed to give her lessons. He couldn't very well teach her anything by going too fast. Which meant he had to take things slow. In the name of education, of course.

SCHOOL'S IN SESSION.

The phrase echoed through Paige's head the moment she heard her doorbell ring the following night, after the longest day of her entire life.

Long because she'd been sweaty and anxious, her condition in no way caused by a lack of air conditioning—Jack had fixed that problem the day before. No, she'd been hot and bothered because of his promise. *Tomorrow.*

The doorbell rang again and her heart lurched.

"This is it," she whispered to herself.

She glanced around her bedroom one final time, her gaze falling on the scarred dresser she hadn't had the money to replace and the chipped mirror that hung above. Her video camera sat in the far corner on top of a neatly folded quilt. Her briefcase sat to the left.

The room looked as it always did, with the exception of the dozen or so candles scattered throughout the area, the black satin sheets—rose petals sprinkled across the slick material—and the champagne chilling on the nightstand. The changes were courtesy of Cosmo and the most recent article she'd read on how to inspire sexy thoughts. She drew in a deep breath and her nipples pressed against the black lace of her floor-length peignoir set—straight out of one of Deb's Victoria's Secret catalogues. One rosy tip peeked through the scalloped pattern and she barely resisted the urge to tug her robe closed. She was doing this. Sure, she'd never been a beauty queen. Never had the personality that made people remember her name. She was average. No better, but certainly no less.

Not bad, she told herself yet again as she fought down a wave of insecurity. Yes, she was armed and ready for a night of sex. She told herself that, but it was still four rings later before she finally made it to the door.

"I was starting to think you'd changed your mind," Jack said when she opened the front door to find him standing there wearing a plaid work shirt and worn jeans that cupped his crotch and clung to his muscular thighs.

His hair was windblown and she had the sudden urge to run her fingers through it, just to see if it felt as soft as it looked.

Her fingers tightened on the doorknob. He was the teacher and she was the student. He led and she followed.

The notion sent a wave of nervous excitement through her. "I haven't changed my mind."

"Good, because..." The words faded as she opened the door more and he got a full glimpse of what she was wearing. His eyes darkened and something flared deep in the depths. Something Paige would have mistaken for passion if she hadn't known better. She'd never stirred passion in any man, much less a man like Jack.

"I've got everything ready." She turned and started for the bedroom.

"Everything?" he asked as he came up behind her. "What's all this?" He glanced at the candle-lit bedroom.

"Sex." As the word left her mouth, heat crept up her neck. "I mean, it's supposed to set the mood for sex, to make me seem sexy."

He stared at her long and hard. "Darlin', it's not about what color your sheets are or how much electricity you can save that makes a woman sexy. Sex appeal comes from inside."

"Please don't say that." She turned and blinked back a wave of tears. "Sex appeal can be learned." That's what Paige wanted to think, what she *needed* to think because, otherwise, she would always be that shy girl who'd worn over-sized T-shirts to bed every night rather than slinky lingerie. She would always be the ignorant virgin who'd cried on her wedding night from the pain and the disappointed look in her husband's eyes. She would always be naive, clueless Paige who hadn't been able to do anything right.

"It *is* inside," he said coming up behind her, so close she could feel the heat from his body. Close, but not touching.

"Meaning you either have it or you don't." She shook her head, noting the strange tingling in her body. He drew that response from her, and at nothing more than his nearness. Because Jack Mission had sex appeal. He stirred women's senses without even trying, wearing nothing more than faded jeans and a work shirt. "I don't have it. I've never had it."

"It's inside all of us. It's our essence."

"I don't have any essence," she said forlornly.

"You don't know you have it, darlin'. Not yet."

She turned and stared up at him. "You really think so?"

"I know so. That's why you asked me for lessons, isn't it? Because you think I know what I'm doing?" She nodded. "Then trust me on this." He took her hands in his. "First off, you need to relax. You're too tense." He opened her hand and massaged her palm.

The touch sent shivers through Paige, followed by a strange sense of warmth that crept through her, easing the fear and worry that knotted her stomach. "That's good," he soothed. "Now you can get started."

A moment of hesitancy went through her at his words, but then she managed to fight her fear back down. She lifted her hand to the top button of her nightgown.

"Hold on." He caught her before she slid the button free. "You're going too fast, darlin'."

"But you said we were going to get started."

"I said you're going to get started." He reached for her video camera sitting on a nearby chair and hefted it to his shoulder. "I'm going to watch, darlin'."

5

JACK REACHED FOR THE LIGHT and a wave of insecurity rushed through Paige.

"No. Leave it off. Please."

He moved the camera and stared at her for a long moment. "Okay," he said after a hesitant second. "For now." He aimed the camera. "Now close your eyes."

"What?"

"Trust me, remember? I'm the teacher, you're the student. Now close your eyes."

She drew in a shaky breath and fought to calm her beating heart. "I don't understand what this has to do with—"

"Sex appeal comes from the inside. You want to learn all about sex, then you need to realize your own sex appeal. You need to feel it, Paige. That's what this is about. It's about feeling. Not seeing or understanding. Just feeling. That's why I want you to close your eyes. So you're not distracted."

She drew in a deep breath and nodded. "Okay."

When her eyelids had fluttered closed, she heard his deep voice. For some reason it seemed huskier, sexier echoing through her head with her eyes clamped so tight. "Listen to the sound of your own breathing," he told her. "Concentrate on the in and out of your breath."

She did as he instructed, feeling the press of her own skin against the lace of her nightgown with every draw of air. The sensation sent a skitter of tingles down her arm and her heart sped faster. She breathed deeper. When the lace snagged on one nipple, she tugged on the material. The pressure sent a delicious jolt through her.

"Now concentrate on the scent of your own perfume."

She inhaled, the scent of apples and cinnamon and warmth filling her nostrils. It was a smell she was all too familiar with, yet it had never seemed quite as mesmerizing as it did with her eyes closed and her own breath echoing in her ears. She inhaled again and again, drinking in the scent and relishing the rush that went through her body.

"Undress."

She wouldn't have obeyed the command, but she was drunk from so many sensations. And excited. She reached for the straps of her gown. Cool air swept across her bare skin as the material pooled at her feet and she stood before him wearing nothing but a pair of slinky panties. Her hands went for those, but his voice stopped her.

"Touch your breast."

The command sent a wave of embarrassment through her, quickly replaced by a rush of excitement. Her heart was pounding too fast, the expectancy in her stomach too fierce to stop now and pull back. She actually wanted to touch herself, to feel her nipple bead with excitement.

At the first stroke of her finger, the tip ripened and sensation unlike anything she'd ever felt before, speared her. She gasped, the sound echoing in the suddenly breathless silence of the bedroom.

"Christ, you're beautiful." His voice, usually so deep and smooth and seductive, came out raw and choked. "Open your eyes, Paige, and look at me."

Her eyelids fluttered open, but she didn't look at him. She looked into the camera poised on his shoulder and saw her own reflection in the small glass lens.

A woman stared back at her, but it wasn't the same woman she faced day after day in the mirror. Her eyes appeared heavy-lidded, her lips parted, the bottom slightly more prominent and slick from the unconscious glide of her tongue. Her breasts were full and flushed, the nipples pebbled. She looked as if she'd just rolled out of bed after a night of wild, hot sex. She looked wild and hot and *sexy*.

He let the camera down and her gaze met his. She saw the desire in his eyes, the heat, the passion, and for the first time in her life, Paige actually *felt* sexy.

Jack Mission—experienced, passionate Jack Mission— wanted her. There was no mistaking the look. No dismissing it as wishful thinking. He was turned on and she was to blame.

She smiled.

"You're sexy, Paige. Sexy as hell." He let the camera down and stepped toward her.

She closed her eyes, fully expecting to feel his arms around her. Instead, she felt the soft press of his lips to her forehead. "Sleep tight."

Her eyes opened in time to see him turn toward the bedroom door. "Where are you going?"

"First lesson's over."

"But I didn't... I mean, we didn't..."

"Not yet." He flashed her a grin. "Sleep tight."

And then Jack Mission did something he'd never done where a woman was concerned. He turned and walked away.

Under any other circumstances, he would have taken her in his arms and loved her within an inch of her life. Quick and to the point. No time for thinking. Just feeling. That had always been his motto. But Paige wasn't his usual type of woman. She was his student and, therefore, entitled to a little patience. His restraint certainly had nothing to do with the fact that almost more than he'd liked seeing her naked, he'd enjoyed the bright-as-a-Texas-sun smile that had lit her face when the truth had sank in.

Almost.

He would take a naked woman over a smiling one any old day. Just not *this* naked one. Not yet, anyhow.

SHE WAS *NOT* HOT.

Paige drew in a deep breath, wiped a drop of perspiration from her temple and walked into the In Touch.

"Call 911," Dolores said the moment she glanced up from her desk. "Somebody's this close to a heart attack."

"Who?" Paige asked as she unloaded her satchel at her desk.

"You," Dolores told her pointedly. "You look hot."

"Flushed," Wally added as he walked by.

"Overheated," Dolores continued.

"I'm fine." Paige blew out a deep breath. "Really."

She wasn't hot. She was late, which was almost as bad. She had five minutes to write up her interview questions for her next appointment—a get-to-know-you talk with the newest resident of the Red Cedar Rest Home.

Late. The word echoed through her head,

sending a wave of dread through her. Paige was never late. She was early. Conscientious. In control. On top of things.

Not this morning. She'd rolled out of bed exactly ten minutes ago. Even after a quick cold shower and three large glasses of ice-cold orange juice, she still felt as if she'd been sitting outside, baking on the pavement.

Thanks to Jack and lesson number one.

He'd gotten her so worked up, so...*ready*, and then he'd walked away.

Which was proof enough that her newly discovered sex appeal hadn't been that potent. Sure, she'd seen the desire in his eyes. She'd even felt the tension in his body, as if he'd been fighting to keep from hauling her into his arms. But then he'd left.

"Why, you're red-faced, dear. Your blood pressure must be sky-high."

"How anybody can even have blood pressure in this weather is beyond me." Paige suddenly noticed the temperature as Wally snuggled deeper into his coat, his earmuffs on, a cup of hot chocolate in his hands.

"It is a mite cold." Dolores pulled her jacket

tighter and shot an accusing stare at Wally. "I told you not to touch the blasted thing."

"I was just lowering the temperature a few notches. After all that heat, I needed to cool off."

"He broke the thermostat at fifty," Dolores told Paige.

"I did not break the thermostat. It's just stuck. But I'm going to pull out my pliers today and see what I can do to fix it."

"I wouldn't do that if I were you."

"It's a simple fix."

"Men." Dolores rolled her eyes. "Now you know why I never remarried after Elias. They're all too stubborn for their own good and I'm too old to be worrying over one of them."

"I'm not stubborn. I'm technically inclined."

"Where have I heard that before?" Dolores turned her attention back to Paige who busied herself booting up her computer.

"Are you sure you're okay? You're awful pink."

"I'm fine. I probably got a little too much sun. I spent most of Saturday at the SAT garage sale. We're trying to raise money to actually buy ourselves a meeting place, or at least be able to lease something. At the activity center, we have to fight with the junior pet owners for chairs every week."

"Wasn't that garage sale in a garage?"

"Yes."

"Then why would you be sunburned?"

"I, um, from going in and out. We had things sitting out in the yard."

Dolores, who had the most watchful eyes in the county, shook her head. "I still say something isn't right. You look hot and tired, like you didn't get much sleep last night."

"Worry," Paige blurted, diverting her eyes from the older woman's knowing gaze. "There's a new girl in the SAT group who's not opening up. I can see she needs to talk, but so far, nothing. I tossed and turned all night." The small measure of truth in the last sentence eased the guilt she felt at lying to Dolores.

"Who's the girl?"

"Jenny Turnover."

"As in Mrs. Walter Jackson Turnover the third?"

"That's the one."

"Honey, it's a miracle she's even going to

your group. Count your blessings. The man's a tyrant. I can't believe he allows it."

"He might not know she's joined the group." She remembered the timid set of Jenny's shoulders, the fear in her dark brown eyes. The uncertainty. "In fact he probably *doesn't* know."

"That's the only explanation I'd believe."

"And he won't know, will he?" She trained her most intimidating glare on Dolores. "Will he?"

"What do you think I am?"

"The biggest mouth in the South, at least according to Deb and most everybody else who reads the In Touch."

"I may have a big mouth, but I know when to keep it shut." At Paige's disbelieving look, she added, "Mum's the word. I swear on my Trinity pin."

Paige nodded. A Trinity pin was the highest award given by the ladies auxiliary to their citizen of the year. Dolores had won hers last year and it held a place of honor above her desk in a glass enclosed frame. If Dolores was swearing on her precious award, she meant business.

"Besides, we women have to stick together.

Speaking of which, I hear Jonas Peabody has been getting very cozy with SueAnn James who works over at the feed store."

"Cozy as in coffee over at Pancake World?"

"Cozy as in the fact that SueAnn has herself an engagement ring the size of Eulie Brown's mouth."

"Get out of here."

"I'm serious. The sucker is huge and I'm headed over to Heavenly Feed to see it." She snatched a disposable camera out of her top drawer. "Can't forget this. Readers want to see, too. I'm betting that Jonas is going to put every man in this town to shame."

Dolores continued to chatter while Paige turned her attention to the subject at hand—her upcoming interview. She needed to put together a list of questions, then finish editing one of Wally's pieces, before getting her buns over to the interview. She had no time to think about Jack Mission and the way he made her feel.

Hot and bothered and...

She shook away the thought and ignored the sudden urge to rush across the room and stand in front of the air unit blowing ice-cold comfort.

She was not bothered in the least by Jack Mission or last night's lesson. And she was *not* hot.

HE WAS HOT.

With the tail of his work shirt, Jack wiped a trickle of sweat from the side of his face and focused his attention on the horse stomping around the corral.

"Don't tell me you're getting back on," Wayne said as Jack started to approach the ornery animal.

"I have to get back on. She's not going to break on her own. Besides, haven't you ever heard the saying about falling off a horse?"

"You didn't fall. You got thrown. Hell, you got *stomped*, boy. Big difference. Not to mention, Molly isn't your typical horse."

Molly was a beautiful thoroughbred who'd been starved and mistreated by her owner's grandchildren—none of whom had known diddly about horses—for the past five years. The owner had suffered from Alzheimer's and had been too sick to care for her, then he'd passed on. Jimmy had come across her a few months back when he'd been scouting out breeding prospects for his stud bull, Valentino. He'd taken one look at the pitiful animal and bought her for a ridiculous amount of money. Jack didn't blame him for forking over the bucks. He would have done the same for Molly. Not because she was a purebred and had the potential to be one of the prettiest horses in the county, but because she'd needed help in the worst way. She'd been neglected, mistreated and hurt. And she was scared.

Scared, he reminded himself, despite the fierce flare of her nostrils and the fact that she looked spitting mad rather than frightened. Her survival instincts had kicked in and she was waging war.

One that Jack intended to win. There wasn't a horse this side of the Rio Grande that he couldn't calm. It was his gift. His passion. The one thing that he did better than anyone else and he took pride in it.

He'd always had a way with animals. While Jimmy had been out riding fence with their father, Jack had been with the horses. He loved to ride, to shoe, to break, to do anything and everything that related to the spirited animals.

It wasn't so much a learned technique that made him so good at what he did. When he was with a horse, he felt a kinship. He felt connected. He *felt* the animal. It was all about feeling.

Just feel.

The phrase echoed through his head, reminding him of last night, of Paige and how beautiful she'd looked with her eyes all dreamy and her full lips parted, her fingertips circling her rosy nipple. It had taken every ounce of strength he'd possessed not to take her then and there.

Hell, he'd wanted to. He'd wanted to carry her to the bedroom and love her fast and fierce. Soon, he promised himself. He was giving her time to adjust, letting her get used to him.

As bold as she'd been when she'd asked him for lessons in the first place, when it came down to actually following through, she was skittish. Inexperienced. Scared, just like Molly.

Jack didn't want her frightened. He wanted her willing in his arms. Completely accepting. Which was why he had no intention of finding himself in her bedroom with all those candles and silk sheets. He'd been hard-pressed, very *hard*-pressed, not to give her exactly what she was asking for. If he meant to go slow, he had to conduct her lessons in more neutral surroundings. The sort of place that didn't inspire any sexual thoughts.

An image of Paige and the way she'd looked last night flashed through his mind again...so soft and warm and luscious.

Okay, so maybe there weren't too many places that wouldn't inspire sexual thoughts. But at least he could take her someplace where he wouldn't be able to act on the lust heating his blood. Someplace where he would definitely have to hold back, until Paige was truly ready for him.

"THE BEDROOM'S THAT WAY," Paige told Jack when he showed up on her doorstep the following night for lesson number two.

He'd knocked, said hello when she answered, given her the once-over with those liquid gray eyes of his, then promptly turned and started back down the walkway.

Paige grabbed her purse, locked the door and hurried after him. "Hey, didn't you hear me?"

"We're not ready for a bedroom yet," he told

her as he straddled the motorcycle and revved the engine. "Climb on."

She straightened her shoulders. "I think I'm ready."

He grinned, his gaze sliding over her, making her wish she could disappear inside the T-shirt dress she was wearing. "Darlin', you're not nearly ready. Don't you have anything a little...tighter?"

She glanced down at her outfit—the waist dropped into a long skirt that ended just above her ankles to reveal the new sandals she'd purchased last month on a shopping trip with Deb. They were a little too strappy for her tastes—she leaned toward a more conservative shoe—but Deb had insisted they looked "hot".

"I thought you said that it didn't matter what I wore. That sex appeal came from the inside."

His grin widened. "You were listening."

"Of course I was listening. I had a perfect GPA in high school and would have graduated at the top of my class."

"You didn't graduate?"

"I finished at night. Back then, Woodrow said he needed me to take care of him full time. So I had to quit, I had too much house stuff to do."

He eyed her for a long moment. "Get on."

"Where are we going? Someplace romantic?"

"Not if I can help it," he said. Or that's what she thought he said, but then the engine drowned out everything as he kicked them into gear and zoomed out of her driveway.

"I HOPE YOU LIKE chicken-fried steak." He sat across from her at Pancake World and handed her a menu.

"I do, but I don't understand what chicken-fried steak has to do with..." She glanced around, noted the elderly couple in the booth next to them, and lowered her voice. "...sex," she finally whispered.

"Consider it foreplay."

"Chicken-fried steak is foreplay? I might be naive but I'm not *that* naive."

"Darlin', man doesn't live by sex alone. I've been working all day, you've been working all day. We need to eat."

But they did much more than just eat over the next hour. They talked. Jack told her about his childhood in Inspiration. About the way he used to tag along after his older brother Jimmy and Jimmy's best friend, Tack Brandon, now a nearby rancher and ex-motocross star. He told her about his love for horses.

In turn, Paige told him about the different classes she was taking, about her job at the newspaper and how she enjoyed writing Deb's Fun Fact column, even though she was still a bit new at it. She talked about her SAT group and how they had to fight with the local pet owners for chairs before every meeting. Her group had been trying to raise money to lease their own meeting place where women could go anytime they needed someone to talk to, and not just on Tuesdays. They talked about their likes and dislikes and the fact that they both loved chicken-fried steak smothered in white country gravy with just a touch of pepper on top.

It was the most pleasant evening she'd had in a long time, and at the same time, the most trying. Paige couldn't calm the sense of expectancy growing in the pit of her stomach. The anxiety. The excitement.

"Aren't you coming in?" she asked, when he dropped her off at home later that evening.

"Not yet," he told her, a grin creasing his handsome face. "I don't think you're ready for that yet."

"Not ready…" The words faded as his meaning hit and her cheeks heated. "I don't think—"

"Don't think," he cut in as he leaned down, his lips a fraction from hers. "Just feel." Then he kissed her.

It was a hot, deep, thorough meeting of tongue and lips that stirred her blood and made her heart pound.

"Open up a little more," he told her and she did as he instructed, giving him better access and playing the dutiful pupil. She lifted her arms when he asked her to do so, slid her hands around his neck and held on to him, pressing her body closer to the hard, muscled length of him.

"That's good," he told her when they both finally came up for air. "Really good."

"I'm ready," she murmured, licking her lips, tasting his essence. "I'm really ready."

"Don't I wish?" He shook his head. "Sleep tight, darlin'." He dropped a kiss on her nose and turned to walk away.

"But I'm *really* ready," she called after him desperately, her heart pounding, her blood rushing.

"Soon," he promised before climbing back onto his bike and riding away.

6

"ARE YOU READY?"

Boy, was she ever. The answer echoed through Paige's head as she stared up at Jack Mission who stood on her front porch. He wore a white T-shirt, faded denim jeans and a smile.

The smile was the kicker. It sent her heart into overdrive and made the rush in her ears. It was the same hungry expression he'd worn the night before last when he'd stared at her through the video lens. As if he really and truly wanted her. All of her. Body and mind and—

"Ready?" he asked again, derailing her dangerous train of thought.

Dangerous? Definitely. Thinking sexy thoughts about Jack Mission wasn't a threat— she could fantasize 'til the cows came home about how he'd nibbled the corners of her lips when he kissed her and how his fingers stroked up and down the length of her spine when he'd pulled her close. No, the danger came in romanticizing about him. Imagining that he really could be attracted to her on more than just a physical level.

She didn't want that. She wanted sex. End of discussion.

She glanced down at the blue jeans and tank top he'd told her to wear. "This doesn't exactly scream seduction to me, but you're the boss."

"That's right. So let's go."

"The bedroom's that way."

"You're moving too fast."

"Look who's talking." She struggled to keep up with him as he led her down the walkway to his bike parked at the curb.

He straddled the seat and motioned behind him. "Climb on."

"Where are we going?" she asked again once they were speeding down the main strip through town.

"Blackjack Cave. It's a secluded little place cut into the side of Brennan's Bluff. When I was a teenager, all the kids used to head up there on Saturday nights. It's a major make-out spot."

Excitement spiraled through her at his words.

She was twenty-six years old and she'd never been to a make-out spot before. Heck, she'd barely been on a date. Woodrow had been her first and only boyfriend and their courting had been limited to sitting on her parents' front porch, eating ice cream on Saturday afternoons. One minute she'd been licking a vanilla cone and the next, she'd been married, saddled with a house to keep and a husband to please.

She hadn't done a very good job at either.

That was then and this is now. The mantra echoed through her head, reminding her that she wasn't the same person.

She had been ignorant and naïve back then. Now she was getting educated, and her next lesson involved a trip to her very first make-out spot.

"So what are we going to do up there?"

A deep chuckle filled her ears and roused her nerve endings. "Why, we're going to make out, darlin'. What else?"

"HOW COME YOUR NAME isn't on here?" Paige held up the candle and stared at the cave wall, decorated with dozens of names carved into the rock. Not just names, but declarations of love. Everything from Sally and Derek to Wayne and Nadine. Some of the young lovers had dates carved beneath their names. Some didn't. Some were even familiar. Paige spotted Pastor Marley and his wife—one of the oldest couples according to the date. It seemed everybody had visited Blackjack Cave at one time or another.

Everyone except for Jack.

Dressed in faded Levi's and a soft white T-shirt, he sat on a blanket in the middle of the dirt floor, his black boots hooked at the ankles. A candle flickered from the mouth of an empty beer bottle. Four unopened bottles of Coors sat in a carrier next to him. He held the fifth in his hand, the glass dripping with condensation. He lifted the drink and downed a mouthful. A drop of moisture chased a slick path over the back of his hand and down his forearm.

"So?" she pressed when he'd finished off the beer and placed the bottle next to the first empty one. "Why isn't your name here?"

Silence ticked by and she had the feeling he was debating whether or not to answer. "Because," he finally said, reaching for beer number three. "I've never actually brought a girl up here."

"Get out of here." She sat down on the blanket next to him and fit another candle into the mouth of the second empty bottle. The twin flames flickered, sending a dance of shadows across the stone walls. "You're kidding, right?"

He twisted the beer top. "I'm serious."

"I find that hard to believe."

He took another swallow and eyed her. "Why's that?"

"Because rumor has it that you've run through more women than Richard Simmons has put out exercise videos."

"Rumor as in my new sister-in-law?"

"As in every single woman in this town. Ruth Jean Paisley has a cousin who lives in New Mexico who says that you were quite a hot commodity up there last year."

He grinned. "You can't believe everything you hear."

"Are you saying it's not true?"

"Not way back when."

"But it's true now."

He shrugged. "I aim to please." His expression eased as he stared into the flames. "Believe it or not, I used to be a one-woman man way back when." His gaze lifted and caught hers. "That's why I've never brought a girl up here. I had a steady when I was a teenager and her daddy didn't take too kindly to her coming up here or going to the drive-in unchaperoned or staying out past ten. He was a judge here in town with a reputation to uphold."

"Judge Baines?"

He shook his head. "Judge Byron McGrew. He's long gone now. He was presiding over Mangrum County the last I heard. But back then, he was as stiff and morally upright as a man could get, with four daughters as wholesome as apple pie."

"Which slice was yours?"

"The youngest."

"What was her name?"

"Gayle." He took another drink. "And the only place we went on Saturday night was to bingo with her folks. Occasionally we headed out to the Dairy Freeze afterward for an ice-cream cone, but most of the time, I just took her home. Sounds boring, huh?"

"Actually, it sounds kind of nice."

"It was." He finished off his beer and reached for another bottle.

"So whatever happened to her?"

"I married her."

"You're *married*?"

"Once upon a time." A look of despair flashed in his eyes before he shrugged and his expression closed. "She passed away a few months after we tied the knot. She had an allergic reaction to a bee sting and didn't make it to the hospital in time. It was a freak thing. She didn't even know she was allergic until it was too late."

For the first time, Paige actually felt a kinship with Jack Mission. She saw a pain she recognized all too well in his liquid gray eyes and it made her want to reach out to him.

Before she could stop herself, she did just that. Her hand covered his. "I'm so sorry."

He didn't move a muscle. He just sat there, her hand atop his. His fingers flexed and she had the feeling he was fighting to keep from turning his hand over and embracing hers.

Crazy, she realized when he pulled his hand away and shrugged. "Don't be. It was a long time ago. All in the past." His gaze caught and held hers. "So what about you? Ever carve your name into the wall of someplace like this?"

She thought about lying, then thought better of it. He knew she was inexperienced. Painfully so. Otherwise, she wouldn't be here. Besides, he'd just shared a part of himself and even though he'd pulled away, she felt compelled to open up to him a little too.

"I never really dated much. Woodrow was my first and only boyfriend and we didn't have many traditional dates. You know, where the boy picks up the girl and off they go to a football game or something. My parents were very strict, too. I was never allowed to go many places with Woodrow, and when I was, it had to be someplace public where my folks could check up on me."

"They sound like good people."

"They were." She blinked against a sudden onslaught of tears, but it was too late. A lone drop escaped from the corner of her eye. She tried to dash it away, but Jack was quicker. His thumb brushed the drop and the feel of his skin against hers sent an echo of heat through her body.

"I'm sorry. It's just, I still miss them a lot."

His hand fell away. "What happened to them?"

"They died in a car accident when I was sixteen." She sniffled. "My life totally changed then. One minute I had a home, the next, I had nowhere to go."

"Didn't you have any family?"

"Just an aunt. My father's sister, but they were never very close. She had her own family—husband number four and half a dozen kids—and didn't want another mouth to feed. Woodrow was the only one who wanted me. My aunt signed a consent form and we got married a month later."

"Would you have married him if things had turned out differently?"

"No. Yes. Maybe." She shook her head. "At the time, if circumstances had been different, I probably wouldn't have married him. But I was young and alone and he said he loved me. He said he would take care of me."

"You don't strike me as the type who needs anyone to take care of you."

"I'm not. Not now. Not ever again."

"So you've given up on finding a 'happily ever after'."

"No. I just think 'happily ever after' implies a fifty-fifty relationship, with both people contributing and both people loving each other equally. It was one-sided with Woodrow and me. I loved him, but he didn't know the meaning of the word. He considered me a possession."

"He was an idiot." The words rang out with such sincerity that a strange sense of warmth unfurled inside her.

"Thanks." She sniffled again and wiped away another traitorous tear. "But can we please talk about something else?"

"Actually," he said, scooting closer to her. "I think we've talked enough. It's time to feel, Paige."

"To feel what?"

"All the heat burning you up from the inside out." He touched her cheek, slid a fingertip down the side of her jaw, the slope of her neck. The contact made her entire body tremble. "Can you feel it?"

She nodded and his hand slid along her collarbone until he reached the strap of her tank top.

He hooked his finger and tugged the strap down just enough to bare one shoulder.

A wave of insecurity washed through her. There were candles, which meant he could see every imperfect inch. She reached up to stop him. As if he sensed her hesitation, he drew away.

"I'm sorry. I'm just not used to all this."

"He didn't love you the way he should have, did he?"

She shook her head. "I don't know." Her gaze met his. "I honestly don't know. He was my first. My only. And it was always over with so quickly."

"He was an idiot," he said again. "A certified idiot. He took from you, Paige. That's all he did. But it's not supposed to be that way. You're supposed to enjoy sex too."

She knew that. The sophisticated woman who read *Cosmo* and took cooking classes knew that, but until that moment, it had never quite sank in. Not until she heard Jack Mission say the words. Until she stared deep into his piercing gray eyes and let him push her back down onto the blanket.

"What do I do now?" she asked once she was flat on her back.

"You don't do anything, darlin'. You simply close your eyes and concentrate on what you're feeling." She heard a beer cap twist and sighed. "Having great sex isn't just about doing the right thing. It's about learning to relax. To free your inhibitions. To *feel*, Paige."

She felt the brush of glass against her bare shoulder and panic skittered through her. "I really don't think this is necessary—"

"Don't think, period. Just feel."

A few heartbeats pounded by before she felt the cold wetness against her mouth. Her lips parted and she felt the trickle of beer on her tongue. The liquid splashed into her mouth and she managed a swallow, but not before the beer spilled over, gliding down her chin and jaw. Her first instinct was to brush it away, but Jack caught her hand.

"No. Feel the sensation."

She balled her fingers and concentrated on the coolness racing across her skin, followed by a rush of warm air as Jack leaned down, his breath flowing over a whisper before she felt the heat of his tongue. He lapped at the wetness and tingles rushed through her body.

Her lips parted, eager to feel his mouth, but he didn't oblige her with a kiss. He licked a few more drops, then leaned up to splash more beer on her neck. The beer slid down her skin and dampened the material of her tank top.

Her nipples pebbled, responding to the cool sensation, begging for more because her skin was on fire from the feel of his tongue, his breath, *him*. He set her ablaze with nothing more than his nearness and she needed something to quench the fire.

He dribbled more beer onto her hard nipples. Her lips parted and a cry vibrated up her throat as she arched toward him. She felt his warm breath on her breast a second before a fierce heat enveloped the ripe crest.

He suckled her through the wet fabric of her shirt, his mouth so hot that it scorched her skin through the material. A wave of embarrassment rushed through her, quickly replaced by desperation. She'd been so worked up all evening, so ready for him to touch her that she couldn't help herself. Her body arched, pressing deeper into the wet heat of his mouth, relishing the incredible feel of him.

He sucked hard and long and deep until she was gasping for air. Just when she could take no more, he pulled away. She felt him lift the edge of her tank top. Beer drizzled onto her bare stomach and pooled in her navel before sliding decadently toward the waistband of her shorts...

The flick of his tongue caught the drop just a fraction shy. He licked her clean before undoing the button of her shorts and inching them down. She tried to tug them back up, but he was persistent and she was hungry and the two didn't make for a good combination.

Besides, it was just candlelight. Not the full brightness of a sixty-watt bulb blazing overhead.

He pulled her shorts free and a few heartbeats later, she felt the cool bottle touch the outside of her thigh. It was a wonderful sensation—the cool glass against her burning skin. He trailed the mouth of the bottle down the outside of her leg, up the inside of her knee, her thigh... Slowly. So maddeningly slowly that her heart nearly gave out in anticipation.

"Can you feel it, Paige? Can you feel every sensation? The rush of your blood? The heat of your skin? The smooth coolness of the bottle?"

She searched for words, but she could only nod, her heart pounding too frantically for logical thought. It felt too good.

"Do you want more?"

She nodded, but it wasn't enough.

"Open your eyes and tell me. Tell me exactly what you're feeling and exactly what you want."

She blinked several times before he finally came into focus through the passion-laden fog that held her captive.

"Tell me."

"I..." She swallowed and fought for a breath. "I feel anxious. Excited."

"Hungry?"

"Very."

"And what do you want?"

"I..." She licked her lips and fought for her voice. "More," was all that finally came out.

"More of this?" He trailed the bottle closer to the heat between her legs, coming close enough to send a rush of electricity skimming through her body. "And this?" Ever so gently, he touched the mouth of the bottle to her hot cleft, swept the cool glass the length of her and she cried out, her eyes closing for a long, delicious moment as her body literally vibrated from the delicious sensations. Another swipe and the pressure built. Her breathing grew ragged and the intensity overwhelmed her.

Her climax hit her hard and fast. It slammed into her, turned her upside down and inside out, robbing her of breath for a frenzied moment.

A few frantic heartbeats later, she heard Jack's voice through the ringing in her ears.

"Look at me," he commanded again and her eyelids fluttered open. "Are you listening to your body? Is it telling you what it wants?" She nodded. "Then tell me, Paige. Tell me exactly what you want right now."

"You," she murmured.

A fierce light fired in his eyes and his muscles tightened. Before she knew what was happening, he leaned over and captured her lips with his. The kiss was fierce, devouring, and lasted all of five frantic heartbeats before he slowed down. The pressure lightened just enough to feed her a much-needed breath and then he deepened the kiss. He kissed her softly, tenderly, thoroughly before he pulled away.

A strange expression lit his eyes, as if he'd just realized what he'd done. He shook his head before taking a mouthful of the beer he'd been tormenting her with.

"Let me guess," she said when she'd finally managed to compose herself. "The lesson's over."

He grinned, but the expression didn't quite touch his eyes or ease the tension that radiated off his body, particularly when his gaze swept the length of hers as she sat there clad only in her panties and a thin tank top. "You're learning, darlin'."

She let out an exasperated sigh and reached for her shorts. "But I'm ready."

"Soon."

Promises, promises.

JACK GRIPPED the handlebars until his knuckles turned white. The insistent throb in his groin urged him to turn his motorcycle around, drive back to Paige's house and relieve himself between her soft, warm thighs.

Instead, he gunned the engine and sent the bike speeding down the main highway, headed for the Mission ranch. Fifteen minutes later, he pulled off his T-shirt and tossed it at the foot of the bed where his suitcase sat open on top of a large chest of drawers, his clothes still packed neatly inside.

Nell had obviously been in doing his laundry. He glanced toward the closet and noted the empty hangers. At least she'd respected his wishes and put everything back in his suitcase the way he liked it. When the restlessness hit him, he liked everything to be ready. That way, he just picked up and walked out. No packing. Nothing to hold him back even a moment longer than he wanted to stay.

He unfastened the button on his jeans, giving his erection a small measure of relief. Not that it helped. He was still hard and throbbing and he wanted her.

Damn, did he want her.

"You're an idiot," he muttered. He could be sleeping like a baby right now. His stress gone. His lust sated. If only he hadn't slowed down back at the cave.

Hell, he'd meant to go full speed ahead. She'd been so ready for him. He'd felt it in the way she'd arched toward him, the way her nipples had hardened at just a glance, the way she'd cried out with her climax and afterward, when she'd whispered the breathless word *you*, when he'd asked her what she wanted.

She did want him, and he wanted her, but then that soft sigh had trembled from her lips. A sound filled with awe and wonder and excitement, reminding him that she was new to all this. So things hadn't turned out quite the way he'd planned.

He hadn't been able to love her fast and furiously.

He hadn't wanted to.

He'd already admitted the truth to himself as he turned off onto the main stretch of highway that led to the Mission ranch. He didn't want to go fast. He wanted to remember the feel of her, to relish every sound she made, to memorize each curve of her body and brand the entire experience into his memory.

Because she was different. While she might not have any romantic notions about him, Paige was still a romantic. Jack couldn't help but admire her optimism after spending years with the jerk she'd had for a husband. While he didn't harbor any fanciful notions when it came to his own future, if Paige truly believed in a happily ever after, more power to her. Jack wasn't about to kill her hope by giving her another wham-bam-thank-you-ma'am experience to add to her already overflowing resume.

He was going to show Paige how thoroughly satisfying sex could be, and that meant keeping a tight rein on his own lust until the time was right. He wanted her to feel every bit like the beautiful, desirable, passionate woman she was. A woman who'd been beaten down for too many years by a senseless jerk who cared about nothing but his own satisfaction.

Just thinking about her ex sent a wave of anger through him. Strange because Jack had never been the jealous type. He didn't let himself get close enough to be jealous. Then again, Paige wasn't his typical woman. She was more, and he was fast learning that he liked her almost as much as he lusted after her.

Not that he was letting emotion cloud his

judgment when it came to Paige Cassidy. Or any woman for that matter. Jack was out of here in a week and a half. He'd be through playing the dutiful brother, and he could go back to living on his own terms. There would be no one waiting for him, no responsibility to anyone except himself and whatever temporary job he decided to take. Just acres and acres of green pasture. Miles of highway. Freedom.

If only the notion sounded half as appealing as it had before Paige Cassidy had walked into his life.

7

HER VERY FIRST ORGASM.

The knowledge played over and over in her head as she closed the door behind Jack and listened to his motorcycle as it peeled away.

Not her very first *orgasm* orgasm. She'd come a long way since Woodrow had walked out of her life. She'd taken a self-exploration class which had not only encouraged her to understand her mind, but her body, as well. No, tonight marked her very first orgasm with a man.

Sort of.

While it had felt good, she still felt restless. Needy. Desperate.

She tossed and turned the rest of the night, only to fall asleep early the next morning and find herself late for work.

Again.

"Is everything all right with you?" Dolores asked when she walked into the office, after three cups of black coffee that hadn't come anywhere close to satisfying the craving she felt deep inside.

"Sure."

"Then you're the only one," Wally said as he walked by wearing a tank top, a pair of shorts and one of those novelty hats that had a palm-sized fan hanging down from the brim. "It's as hot as Hades in here. I swear I'm filing suit against Deb when she gets back. These are unbearable working conditions."

"Oh, hush up," Dolores told him. "It's your own fault. Jack fixed it."

"We went from one pole to the next. My teeth were chattering. I had to try to adjust the thermostat."

"You just had to break it."

"I didn't actually break it. I relocated it. My hands were trembling so bad from the cold that I couldn't help but knock it off the wall. Technically, the tile floor is to blame for the thing shattering."

"All I know is that I can put on a coat, but I can't exactly strip naked," Delores said. She seemed thoughtful for a moment. "On second thought, I guess I could. I mean, it's no different than a nude beach—"

"Don't even think it."

"Then hand over your hat fan."

"But I had to special order this thing from a catalogue and pay extra to have them overnight it to me."

"The hat fan or I start taking it all off." To emphasize her point, Dolores did a little shimmy and hummed the tune to The Stripper.

"Okay, okay," Wally said when she reached for the second button on her blouse. "But I want it back when the stupid thing is fixed."

"We'll see." Dolores plopped the hat on her head, turned the fan on high and sat down at her desk.

Meanwhile, Paige was suffering from her own form of heatstroke that had nothing to do with the temperature and everything to do with Jack.

Not because she actually liked him. Sure, he was nice to talk with and they had things in common—they'd both been married, both lost one or more parents and both enjoyed a good chicken-fried steak over at Pancake World—but that wasn't the reason she was so anxious to see him.

She simply took her studies seriously. Nothing more. She certainly didn't want Jack Mission.

SHE WANTED JACK MISSION.

Paige admitted the truth to herself as she stood in line at the Tasty Freeze that night and watched Jack buy a double scoop cone and hand it to the small, bratty child who'd been playing with his own cone and dropped it. Paige—a self-proclaimed child lover and future mother wannabe had wanted to wring the little boy's neck, but not Jack. He'd taken the boy aside, whispered a few words that had calmed the devil child into a smiling angel and then stepped in line to buy the kid another.

He took the double chocolate dipped cone and knelt beside the child. Jack's large, work-roughened fingers dried the boy's stray tears and fluffed a few locks of blonde hair, and Paige's heart flipped.

He was handsome and sexy and nice, and she'd never wanted a man as much as she wanted Jack at that moment.

Not in a love sense, she quickly reminded herself. Not the 'til death do us part, I promise to love, honor and cherish sort of love that a woman felt for her one and only. No, what she felt for Jack was purely infatuation. A crush. Like the time she'd fallen for Mister Jenkins, her eighth grade English teacher. He'd been a major hunk, and had stirred her hormones into a frenzy. He'd also been nice and had graciously helped her with her grammar when she'd been having trouble. He'd appealed to her on a sexual and a human level, and she'd been determined to marry him. Of course, she'd gotten older and the infatuation had faded.

"You're good with kids," she said when he turned to hand her a cone.

"Thanks. It's no different than dealing with an ornery colt. They'll both kick you if you give 'em your backside. You just have to be calm and in control."

"You'll make a good dad someday."

"Someday far, far away."

"So you're not after the wife and proverbial two point five kids."

"I think the statistic's probably changed, but

no, I'm happy just the way I am. What about you?" he asked.

"I'd like to get married again. To the right man. And I'd make sure it would be the right man this time."

"Right, as in?"

"Permanent. A man who's home when he's supposed to be. A man who wants kids and will be there forever. The right man is definitely a forever sort of man." She eyed him as they walked to a nearby table. "I guess forever gives you the creeps, huh?"

"I wouldn't go that far." He grinned. "Just a bad case of hives. So tell me, what happened with Woodrow?"

"He left me for another woman. Actually, he left me for several different women."

"The guy was a jerk," he told her as he held out a chair for her. "A real jerk."

"He just wasn't what I thought he was. I'm not angry with him. I mean, I am sometimes, but overall, I'm grateful that he left. Who knows if I would have found the courage to walk out on my own."

"You would have," he told her as he seated

himself across from her. "You're a strong woman. You would have."

"I like to think that, but..." She shook away the rush of insecurity and tried to concentrate on the here and now.

Jack handed her a napkin, his fingertips brushing hers, and electricity shimmied through her body.

Yep, a good, old-fashioned crush, and everyone knew that crushes were healthy. So long as the "crusher" didn't get any unrealistic notions about the "crushee," and Paige certainly had no misconceptions when it came to Jack.

He was a tutor, plain and simple, trading his knowledge for some extra cash. Otherwise, a man like Jack Mission never would have come within spitting distance of Paige. She'd never been a raving beauty, never attracted men in droves the way some girls did. She'd always been plain. Average.

She glanced down at the shorts and matching shirt she wore. It was a far cry better than the baggy jeans and oversized T-shirts she'd lived in less than six months ago. But her attire still wasn't anything flashy.

Not like the woman wearing a halter top and miniskirt who sat at a nearby table and smiled when Jack caught her eye. He smiled back and dread settled in Paige's stomach because it solidified the truth—Jack Mission didn't go for average.

Men like Jack, handsome, made-for-sex men like Jack went for long legs and big bosoms, like the halter top woman. The type of female she could never be, no matter how many self-improvement classes she took. Not that she *wanted* to be such a woman. She wanted a man to love her for who she was, on the inside as well as the outside. A man who would be there for her always.

By his own admission, always wasn't a part of Jack's vocabulary.

Even so, her heart fluttered when he straddled a chair across from her, an ice-cream cone in his hand, and turned his full attention on her.

He took a lick of his vanilla cone and grinned. "So you like ice cream?"

"I don't see how you giving me bedroom lessons has anything to do with eating ice cream."

"Being good in the sack is all about being sensual. You have to be in tune with yourself, with each of your senses. Sight, sound, smell, touch, *taste*."

"I doubt the fact that I'm eating strawberry ice cream will make me good in bed."

"I don't know. With a little strawberry ice cream strategically placed..."

His meaning sank in and her cheeks heated. She refused to let her embarrassment get the best of her, however. "Then let's grab a pint and head back home."

"A pint? Darlin', try a half gallon."

Not knowing what to say, she kept her mouth shut and concentrated on eating. Not a difficult task with Jack sitting across from her, his hard thigh pressed against hers beneath the small table. His tongue flicked out to scoop some ice cream and her heart jumped.

"What's the matter?" he asked, after taking a long lick. "You okay?"

"F-fine." But she wasn't fine. She was hot and hungry and she needed more than an ice-cream cone. She needed his kiss, his touch, his taste. Yes, she wanted to taste him more than she wanted her next breath.

The next fifteen minutes passed painfully slowly. She swallowed the last of her ice cream and watched with relief as he pushed his chair back, signalling that it was finally, *finally* time to go.

In her eagerness to get to the parking lot, she ran into a nearby table. A milk shake took a tumble and spilled across the metal top.

"I'm sorry..." The words died as her gaze locked with Jenny Turnover's. "Hi, Jenny."

"Um, hi."

"You know my wife?" The question came from the gentleman seated across from her.

Paige turned and found herself face-to-face with Jenny's husband, who looked none too pleased that she'd said hello.

"Aren't you the girl from the newspaper? The one who writes those Fun Fact columns."

"Why, yes."

He frowned. "I hate those columns. Talk about destroying the moral fiber of this country. It's people like you who corrupt our youth."

"Mr. Turnover, my column is strictly for fun. The single women in town get a kick out of it."

"And they're liable to stay single because of it. What a cockamamie bunch of nonsense."

"Is there a problem?" The question came from Jack, who'd just come up behind Paige. His intense gaze zeroed in on Mr. Turnover.

"Just the breakdown of our society."

"Glad to hear it's nothing too serious. You ready?"

Paige fought to keep the smile from her face, but it appeared anyway. Walter Turnover's frown deepened.

"Come on, Jenny. We're leaving."

"But she's getting me another shake—"

"Now." He took her hand and hauled her after him. "I'll not have you associating with people like that. Why, that woman is feeding the moral decline of our nation..."

As Paige watched Jenny follow her husband to the car, a scene flashed in her head. She saw herself as she'd been so long ago, following in Woodrow's footsteps, going along with whatever he said, doing whatever he said, enduring whatever he said. Jenny's husband didn't do anything more severe than hold her firmly by the arm, but it went beyond any physical abuse.

This was mental, emotional abuse, and on some levels it was even worse than getting punched or slapped because it didn't just break bones. It broke a woman's spirit.

Paige caught Jenny's eyes and did the only thing she could. She smiled, a heartfelt, genuine smile to let the other woman know that Paige was there for her.

"Are you okay?" Jack's deep voice reached her ears, followed by the strong touch of his fingers on her arm as he came up next to her.

"I just remembered something."

"What?"

"How thankful I am that I'm divorced. Do you know that guy?"

"I know him from way back. He's always been a little conservative, but this isn't like him." Jack watched as they walked away. Maybe he and Walter needed to have a little talk.

"Is he mean?" Paige said, interrupting his thoughts.

"I don't know about that, but he doesn't look exactly nice now, does he?" He stared at the couple and watched as Walter hauled Jenny around and literally shoved her inside the car.

"Don't." Paige touched his arm. "You'll only make things worse."

"Punching him out for manhandling a lady will make things worse? I'm banking it will make me feel a whole lot better."

"You, but not her. You'll make it worse for her."

"I'd be helping her."

"You can't help her until she wants help. She doesn't. Not yet."

But hopefully she would want that help soon. She'd taken the first step by showing up at an SAT meeting, not once but twice now. If only she made it to a third.

Paige would find out tomorrow.

Until then...

"Where are we going?" she asked, sliding her arms around Jack's waist and holding tight as he steered them down the main strip through town. "The bedroom?"

"Not yet."

"I'm getting tired of hearing that."

"Then stop asking."

They ended up at the football stadium, the stands deserted, the field dark. "Why are we here?"

"For a little privacy," he said, pulling her off

the bike and directing her toward the seats. "It's basketball season and the football players don't start practicing for another few weeks."

"Wouldn't we have more privacy at home?"

"It's not about privacy. It's about freeing your inhibitions and relaxing. You worry too much about the little things. It doesn't matter where you are or what you wear. Sex is mental, Paige."

"You keep saying that, but I get the impression you're avoiding the bedroom on purpose." She stared into his eyes, searching for an answer. Were her instincts right or was she just being paranoid?

Maybe he was avoiding the bedroom on purpose because he didn't want to get intimate with her. Maybe her ignorance was too much of a turn-off and he hadn't found a way to let her down easy. Maybe…

The endless *maybes* faded as Jack pulled her close and kissed her.

Her lips parted instinctively and he pushed his tongue deep, stroking and tasting and stirring her senses into a frenzy. His deep breaths filled her ears. The scent of him inflamed her senses. His nearness set her entire body on fire.

A wet heat pooled between her legs. Her skin came alive, ultrasensitive as she concentrated on truly *feeling* as Jack had instructed her. She felt everything—the night wind whispering over her skin, the hard wood of the bleacher seat at her back, the solid warmth of the man pressing into her, the heat of his fingertips as he worked at the button on her jeans.

Soon the material slid free and she found herself wearing nothing but her T-shirt and panties. A quick swipe of cotton, and he pulled the shirt up and over her head, tossing it to the ground with the rest of her clothes.

She covered her breasts with her arms, but Jack was there, pulling her hands aside so that he could look. Her heart pounded with a sudden panic, but she soothed herself with the fact that it was dark. There was nothing but moonlight to illuminate her less than perfect body.

Jack's gaze deepened and she knew that he liked what he saw. The knowledge sent a wash of satisfaction through her that quickly faded into excitement as he leaned down and his mouth closed over one nipple.

He sucked on her, catching the ripe peak between his teeth, lapping with his tongue until she forgot all about her naked state and became conscious only of Jack and what he was doing to her.

Too much and at the same time, not nearly enough.

"Please," she gasped and he obliged, kissing a path down her belly to the wet heat between her legs.

He parted her legs, fingertips sliding over the soft skin of her thighs, bringing her nerve endings to life. He moved his hands over her thighs, up and around until his large fingers slid beneath her buttocks. He drew her to him, spread her legs even wider and then he touched the wet heat between them. She arched toward him at the first lap of his tongue.

He stroked her, sliding his rough fingertip over the softness of her skin before plunging it deep inside. The pleasure almost made her shatter, and she fought to drag air into her lungs. He stroked and explored until she squirmed, and then he put his mouth fully on her.

The shock of feeling his kiss at her most private place sent a bolt of panic through her.

Woodrow had never kissed her there. She reached for Jack's head, suddenly desperate to pull him away and beg him to stop, but somehow her hands had a different idea. Her fingers threaded through the dark silk of his hair, holding him closer, urging him to continue.

He tasted and savored, his tongue stroking, plunging, driving her mindless until she came apart beneath him in a shattering climax more intense than the first one she had with him less than forty-eight hours ago. A cry vibrated from her throat and before she could stop it, she heard her high-pitched wail split open the quiet night.

It was sometime later before she finally managed to open her eyes. She found Jack stretched out on a nearby bleacher, staring at the sky overhead. Disappointment filled her. She was lying there stark naked and exposed and he wasn't even looking. At the same time, she felt a small measure of relief.

Taking the opportunity, she reached for her clothes.

"Did you like it?" His words stopped her in the middle of tying one shoe and she glanced up. He didn't look at her. His attention was still fixed on the sky.

"Um, yes. It was..." Fantastic. Fabulous. Earth-shattering. "Nice," she finally said, not wanting to turn him off even more after her shameless response. She'd nearly screamed, for heaven's sake.

She expected him to make some comment, to grin or tease or do something to make her blush. Instead, he stood and reached for her hand. "Come on. We'd better get going."

Paige forced her wobbly legs to move as she followed him down the bleacher steps and wished with all her heart that he would say something—anything to give her some clue as to what was running through his head. Had her response disappointed him? Excited him? Angered him? Was she as totally inept at having an orgasm as she'd been at everything else in her life?

Say something, she silently begged, but Jack only directed her onto the back of the waiting motorcycle.

He gunned the engine, shoved the bike into gear and off they went.

Paige held onto him and did her best to concentrate on the hum of the motorcycle, the rush of wind, anything but the doubts racing through her mind.

Instead, all she could think about was what she'd done wrong.

THE ONLY THING WRONG with Paige was the fact that despite the cold shoulder he was giving her, she still wanted Jack Mission. The ride home only fed the need inside her and by the time she climbed off the bike, she was this close to jumping his bones right there on the sidewalk in front of her house.

She managed to wait until they reached the front door.

"Sleep tight—"

"Don't even think it."

"What are you talking about?"

"I'm ready."

"Darlin', we've been over this before. Not—"

"—yet," she finished for him. "I'm sick of hearing that. I'm ready. I've been ready for ages. I'll never be more ready."

"Okay."

"And if you give me more of the same bull about how I'm not, I'm liable to give you a roundhouse kick right to your midsection. I took a six-week self-defense course in karate a few months ago and I'm damned good—what?"

"I said okay. You're ready. Let's go."

"You're kidding, right?"

"Darlin'." He grabbed her hand and placed it over his throbbing groin that literally jumped at her touch. "Do I feel like a man who's kidding?"

"No, you definitely mean business."

"Good. Now I think it's time we gave those silk sheets a try, otherwise we could always stay out here and try out the porch swing."

"The bedroom is good."

And before he could change his mind, Paige grabbed him by the hand and led him inside. It was finally time.

8

PAIGE WASN'T SURE how they made it to the bedroom. Whether Jack led her or she led him or they both rushed for it. She only knew that seconds later they were standing next to her bed and he was kissing her.

Desperation seemed to drive him for the first few moments of contact, then something happened. The kiss slowed, deepened as Jack seemed to relax, as if he had all night. As if he wanted to make each moment count. He teased and stroked her with his tongue, stirring the heat inside her body until she was flushed and breathless and needy.

She whimpered and he swept her into his arms and carried her toward the bed. But he didn't release her right away. Instead, he held her, his mouth feasting on hers, his fingers burning into her body. Then he lowered her to her feet in a long, slow glide down the fierce heat of his hard, aroused body.

Paige wasn't sure what happened to their clothes. One minute she was wearing her favorite flower print skirt and blouse and the next, she lay on the bed wearing nothing but her bra and panties. Jack loomed over her, wearing only his jeans, the button undone, the zipper straining over a huge erection that looked ready to bust out at any moment.

His gaze held hers for a long moment. Then he moved his attention lower, sweeping the length of her body. A wave of insecurity washed through her and she reached to cover herself.

"No." He caught her hands and urged them to her side. Suddenly, as much as she wanted to cover herself, she wanted even more to feel his bare body against her own.

He unhooked her bra and swept her panties down her legs, leaving her naked against the soft sheets. Moonlight spilled from the window, illuminating the room in a faint light that sculpted Jack's features and eased her own hesitation.

Moonlight she could handle. Moonlight was

flattering. Moonlight hid the flaws and lent a softness to everything it touched.

Her fears eased, only to be replaced with an excitement as Jack slid the zipper of his pants down. His erection sprang into her palm, huge and hard and throbbing. His skin stretched tight as he slid into her tight grip and a gasp rumbled from his throat.

"I'm definitely ready," he murmured, the words raw and husky.

"But I'm the one who's supposed to be ready."

He stared down at her, his gaze intense and consuming. "Then let's see if you really are, darlin'."

He touched her breast, plucked and pulled at the nipple until it puckered and throbbed. His hand slid lower, gliding over the quivering flesh of her stomach to tangle in the patch of red curls at the base of her legs. His fingers slid into her slick flesh and she shuddered.

The touch was softer than when he'd stroked her with the bottle. Warmer. More purposeful. She couldn't help the raw moan that slid past her lips and filled the breath-laden silence that surrounded them.

Skin met skin as he settled over her, blocking out everything except the sight, the sound, the smell of him. His eyes glittered like pools of silver. Rasping breaths parted his sensual lips. The steamy scent of sex, heat and aroused male filled the air. Muscle corded his body, flexing and bunching with every movement.

He kissed her again, tasting and sucking her tongue until every nerve in her body came alive. Strong hands roamed over her, arousing every nerve, making her want and crave him in a way more intense than anything she'd felt before.

He slid down her sweat-dampened body, his lips closed over her nipple and he sucked with a fierce sweetness that actually brought tears to her eyes.

Woodrow—especially Woodrow—had never touched her with such gentleness. He'd never seduced or stirred *anything*. He'd only taken his own pleasure. *Taken* because she'd never been able to give. She'd never known how.

"Tell me what to do."

"Just look at me, darlin'." He caught her gaze and held it. "Just look and feel." He paused. "You're protected?"

At her nod, he gratefully urged her legs apart. The voluptuous head of his penis nudged her slick opening, pushing in, stretching. With one smooth thrust he filled her. He rested his forehead against hers for a long moment, as if he needed to catch his breath.

He moved his hips the tiniest bit and heat fluttered through her. She rotated her pelvis, giving him better access, begging him for more.

He flexed his buttocks and began to move slowly, penetrating deeply, thoroughly. His hands roamed over her body, stirring her on the outside the way his sex stirred her on the inside. He sucked and licked her nipples and drove her wild with each and every thrust.

The pressure built inside her. Higher, higher. Faster, faster. And then it happened. The heavens parted and the earth shook and Paige Cassidy had the most incredible orgasm of her entire life.

"That's it, baby," he groaned. "Let it go."

Her body tightened, milking his, wringing a deep groan from him. He plunged once, twice, burying himself as deep as he could go as he followed her over the edge.

Jack collapsed on top of her, their hearts thundering in perfect sync, their chests heaving and pressing against each other with each frantic breath.

How was it?

Paige wanted so much to ask the question, to know what Jack was thinking as he lay there atop her, but she couldn't voice the words. As much as she wanted to know, she didn't dare ask for fear of the answer. So instead, she slid her arms around him and closed her eyes. And for the first time since she'd met Jack Mission, she actually fell right to sleep.

JACK WATCHED PAIGE SLEEP and tried to make some sense out of the feelings pushing and pulling inside him.

He hadn't meant to make love to her tonight. He'd meant to touch her and taste her, but the episode at the football stadium should have been the end of it. Only things had turned out differently—because she was different.

She was more than a pretty face. She was nice and smart and she actually blushed when he said something risque. The women he usually kept company with—the safe women who knew the score and were only out for a good time— had stopped blushing a long time ago. She was also caring and compassionate. He could still remember the look on her face as she'd stared after Jenny Turnover. She truly wanted to help the woman.

But even more than being a good person, Paige appealed to him on a deeper level.

Never had a woman made him feel so… Hell, just *feel*. That was the trouble with her. She didn't just turn him on on a physical level. She touched him emotionally.

She changed everything he thought he knew about sex. Sex was sometimes slow and easy. Sometimes fast and fierce. But never had it been like it was with Paige, so wondrous and new, so exciting and *intense*. Never had Jack wanted to lose himself inside a woman and brand her as his own so that no other man touched her ever again. *Ever*.

He wasn't possessive. He never had been, even with his first wife. She'd been his first love and he'd been crazy about her, but he'd never felt the all-consuming rush he felt when he looked at Paige. He wanted to wrap her in his arms and shield her from the world as much as he wanted to bury himself deep inside her hot slick body and not come up for air until he'd had the fiercest, most powerful climax of his life. Crazy. Yet the feelings were there and he could no more ignore them than he could roll out of bed and leave her at this moment.

But he *would* leave because that's what Jack did. He blew through town until he grew bored and people got a little too close. Then he moved on. He was always wandering.

No matter how much he suddenly wanted to stop.

"YOU DEFINITELY LOOK HOT today." Dolores's words met Paige the minute she walked into the In Touch office the next morning after the most incredible night of her life.

Make that educational. Last night had been purely a learning experience, and a stellar one at that.

Of course, if it just happened to be an incredible learning experience, then that just made things all the better. Everyone knew that when one enjoyed their education, they gave it their all.

"Actually, I'm not feeling hot at all." Or frustrated. Or needy.

The only thing she did feel was curious, and a little scared. She and Jack had gone on to make love several more times after the first earthshattering experience, but not once had they actually talked about what they'd done. Paige had meant to ask him this morning for a progress report. She'd promised herself last night that she'd find out what he thought, but he'd already left by the time she'd opened her eyes.

"Besides, it actually feels normal in here today." Paige glanced at the new thermostat on the wall.

"And let's hope it stays that way." Dolores shot a glare at Wally before turning her attention back to Paige. "As for you, I mean hot as in *hot*." Dolores swept an appreciative glance over Paige. "My, my, but you're all dressed up. Is that new?"

"This old thing?" Paige glanced down at her flower print sundress, a little shorter and tighter than she normally wore, but it fit her mood today. The material was light and airy, the color vibrant.

That's how she felt today. Vibrant. Ready to tackle even the toughest job.

"You have to interview Bea Cromwell today."

On second thought. Her stomach did a somersault as she turned to face Wally. "I have to interview who?"

"Bea Cromwell. You know, tall old lady with blue hair and a mean streak."

"I was afraid that's who you'd said." Bea Cromwell was the meanest, nastiest eighty-five-year-old to ever play a Bingo card over at the senior's center. She gossiped. She cussed. She chewed tobacco. And she spit, so heaven help the person who happened to be in her way. The only reason anyone tolerated her was because she just happened to be one of the wealthiest women in town.

"You're kidding, right?"

Wally sneezed so loud the cup on his desk rattled. He bundled into his sweater. "I've got a cold and I'm freezing."

"But it's hot in here today."

"That's what's getting to me. One day it's hot. The next it's cold. I've got a fever."

"Your own fault," Dolores reminded him. "I told you to leave the thermostat alone."

"I didn't listen. There. Are you happy?"

"Not nearly. I want you to say, Dolores, you were right."

"Dolores, you were right."

"Dolores, you told me not to touch the thermostat, but I was stubborn."

"Dolores, you told me not to touch the thermostat, but I was stubborn."

"I promise never to be stubborn again."

"I promise never to be stubborn again."

"Dolores, I'm truly sorry."

"Dolores, I'm truly sorry."

"Dolores, you're a goddess. And beautiful. And—"

"—a pain in the ass."

"A know-it-all pain in the ass," Dolores reminded him. "And don't you forget it."

"I hate you," he muttered to the older woman before pausing to blow his nose.

"The feeling's mutual, sugar. Toodooloo," she said, waving her fingers as she gathered up her purse. "I've got a hair appointment and then a luncheon."

"Please," Wally begged once Dolores had disappeared. "You have to do this for me. Deb's had it scheduled for two months and I promised her I wouldn't let her down."

"I've got my own interviews and I need to finish up two articles."

"I'll do the articles. You just go." He grabbed her purse and handed it to her. "Please."

"But—"

"The only reason she agreed to this is that she gets her picture in the paper. While she's mean, she's also vain. You can't miss it and you can't be late. She's a stickler for being on time."

"But—"

"I'll clean your desk."

She straightened the stack of papers and sighed. "My desk is already straight."

"I'll buy you lunch."

She reached into her satchel and produced a brown paper bag. "I brought my own."

He glanced around as if searching before his eyes lit on her feet. "Those shoes have got to be killing you. Tell you what, you do the interview and bring me back some cough medicine from the pharmacy and I'll give you a grade A foot massage."

Paige eyed the high-heeled sandals she'd dared to put on that morning. Her toes ached at just a glance and she'd only been wearing the blasted things for forty-five minutes. "You're on. But—" she poked him in the chest with her finger "—if she spits on me and ruins this dress, you're paying the dry-cleaning bill."

"It's a deal." He handed her a stack of notes and settled down at his desk.

Paige ignored her aching feet, grabbed her satchel and interview pad and headed down the stairs. At least now she had a distraction, one she needed in the worst way. Otherwise, she'd be stuck at her desk, worrying and wondering what Jack Mission thought about last night.

Was he glad, sad, angry, indifferent? Had she been a total failure last night, the way she'd been most of her life? Or had he been pleased with her progress? Or was he, at the moment, trying to figure a way out of their arrangement?

She forced the questions aside and started down the stairs. It didn't matter. Even if he called it quits right now, she would still come out of the agreement much wiser than when she'd started. She'd learned a great deal over the past week.

Of course, most of what she'd learned involved her own likes and dislikes. The way she liked to be touched, stroked, kissed. He hadn't actually told her how to touch him, to stroke him, to kiss him…

"Hey, there, uppity up." Jack's deep voice stopped her at the foot of the stairs. She stared across the small alleyway that ran between the grocery store and the newspaper office. He wore jeans and a faded denim work shirt open to reveal a white T-shirt beneath. For a split second, an image flashed through her mind the way he'd looked last night as he'd loomed above her.

He'd been beautiful, his body hard and powerful and tanned from hours spent outdoors. Gold hair sprinkled his chest and swirled around his flat, brown nipples. Muscles rippled as he braced his arms and flexed his body and plunged deep. So very deep…

"You look hot." His deep voice pushed past the sensual fog holding her prisoner and jerked her back to reality.

"It's the dress. I don't usually wear this sort of thing and I never would have bought it, but Deb talked me into it. She said the cut was flattering—"

"I mean hot as in temperature hot, darlin'. You're sweating."

At his words, she became acutely aware of the glide of perspiration near her temple and she reached up to slap the wetness away.

"I'm sorry, I thought...I mean, Dolores said the same thing, but she meant..."

"But you do look hot, too." A grin curved his features as his gaze swept the length of her. "I do like the dress. You actually have legs."

She couldn't help herself. She grinned and the tension eased. "Yes. They're good for walking."

"And holding on." His words brought memories of last night flooding back, but Paige was determined not to be sidetracked again.

Fighting back the memories, she adjusted her purse on her shoulder. "So what are you doing here? Shouldn't you be at the ranch?"

"I was at the ranch, and I'll be heading back after I pick up a load of feed over at Murphy's. But first—" he took a bite and swallowed before pitching the core into a nearby trash bin "—I wanted to see you."

A sense of dread filled her because she'd faced too many morning afters and none had ever gone well. Most had been spent with Woodrow running through a list of her shortcomings and what she'd done wrong.

Everything.

"We're not scheduled to see each other until tomorrow night," she blurted. She didn't want to hear this. She didn't need to hear it.

"That's what I wanted to see you about."

Here comes the brush-off.

"We have a deal."

"But it's not going to work the way that it stands."

"You agreed to tutor me," she pointed out. "You promised you'd teach me everything you know every Monday, Wednesday and Friday for the duration of two weeks."

"I know, but if you want the job done right, then I think we need more lessons."

"You can't just back out because—what did you say?"

"I want to see you tonight." He crossed the distance to her. "Every night, until Deb and Jimmy make it back."

Elation jolted her at the same time a wave of disappointment rushed through her, filling her with a sense of dread that was all too familiar. "I was that bad last night."

"Are you kidding?" He caught her chin and tilted her face up until her gaze met his. "Darlin', you were that good. I'm just taking my responsibility seriously. You deserve more than a crash course. I want to take my time and do this right. I don't want to leave anything out."

"I wouldn't want you to do that." This time, she was the one who actually reached out and kissed him because for the first time in her life, Paige Cassidy didn't feel like a failure.

She felt like a woman. A real woman.

9

THE NEXT FEW DAYS PASSED in a dizzying blur. Paige spent her days at the newspaper and her nights with Jack. Every night, just as he'd said.

He was every bit the experienced teacher she'd known he would be. The man was a sex machine. He could set her ablaze with just a glance and, as she soon discovered, she could do the same to him. It was all about the little things. A simple gesture such as the lick of her lips, the bat of her eyes, the sultry sway of her hips and bam, he was ready.

She'd expected the seduction process to be more complicated, but with Jack it seemed easy. Natural.

If Paige hadn't know better, she might have thought she'd met her soul mate. But she knew better, of course. While he was an expert lover, so in tune to every sound she made, every breath she took, he wasn't the sort of man a girl let herself fall in love with. Not unless she wanted to end up with a broken heart.

Paige had already had hers shattered and she wasn't risking that ever again. It had taken her too long to glue all the pieces back together.

Woodrow had been the temporary sort. The good-looking, good-time guy that every girl lusted after. Paige had made the mistake of thinking that his interest was more than lust. That when he looked at her, he had the same hopes and dreams that she had.

She knew now that she'd only been a challenge. The classic good-girl virgin, who ended up being nothing more than a conquest. Sure, he'd gone further than simply talking her out of her panties in his back seat. He'd married her, but that, too, had been selfishly motivated. Every other woman in town had seen him for exactly the man he was. Everyone but Paige. She'd been younger and so easy to please. That's why he'd married her. He'd wanted a housekeeper and a cook. But he'd gotten a surprise. She hadn't been any good at either, and so he'd gone looking elsewhere.

She could keep house now and cook and she

wasn't the fashion disaster she'd been way back when, but she wasn't everything a man like Jack Mission needed in his life or in his bed. He needed an equal and despite the fact that Paige told herself she was just that, she didn't truly feel it inside.

Not that it mattered. Even if she was every bit the desirable woman she sometimes felt like, Jack still wasn't the right man for her.

She would never find herself saying "I do" to a man like her ex ever again.

No matter how good he was in bed. Or how he held her hand when they went to the movies or fed her French fries off his plate when he met her for lunch or encouraged her when she spoke about her SAT group and her endeavors to find a permanent meeting place so that the women actually had someplace safe to go when their home lives overwhelmed them.

Never again.

"LEAVE THE LIGHT OFF." Paige's command reached Jack's ears as he leaned back and reached for the lamp on the nightstand. Her hand closed over his an inch shy of his target. "Please."

"I want to see you."

"You can see me just fine. The street light's blazing outside." A nervous laugh bubbled from her lips. "I practically need sunglasses."

"It's just a small lamp."

"It's more romantic this way," she blurted, her grip tightening on his hand. Her eyes glittered with panic, and a surge of protectiveness spread through him. A feeling he fought down. While she'd been so open to him the past few nights, loving and eager and so damned giving, he sensed that she was holding back.

That there was something holding her back.

"*Please*. It's..." She licked her lips and he knew her mind searched for a plausible excuse. "It's more romantic with the lights off."

"Why don't you tell me what's really bothering you?"

"I don't know what you're talking about."

"You're afraid."

"Afraid? Of you?"

"For me to see you with the lights on. You're scared I'll see the real you, and that I won't like what I see."

"That's crazy." Despite her words, he could

tell that he'd touched a sensitive spot. Her eyes brightened with tears and an ache gripped his chest.

"Baby, don't let him do this to you. He's long gone. You don't have to be afraid."

"I'm not." She shook her head frantically and a fierce light fired in her eyes, as if she fought the truth. "I'm not afraid of anything."

"You are."

"Look who's talking." Her fierce gaze caught and collided with his. "When's the last time you stayed longer than a few months in one place?"

"This isn't about me." He pulled away from her and swiveled to sit on the side of the bed.

"You want to talk fear." She scrambled to a sitting position behind him. "Then let's talk."

"I didn't have talking in mind when I came in here. I just want to see you."

"You're not restless," she rushed on as if he hadn't said a word, or rather, she wanted to pretend he hadn't said a word. Because then the talk wasn't about her. It was about him. "You're afraid to stay too long in one place."

"You're changing the subject, and for your information, I don't *like* staying too long in one place."

"The subject is fear. You're afraid to plant roots."

"We're talking about *your* fear, and I don't need roots."

"Afraid to get too close."

A grin curved his lips. "Darlin', we've been about as close as two people can get."

"That's physical. I'm talking about more."

"You're the one who wanted sex lessons. Sex implies physical."

"You don't wake up with me. You stay most of the night, but you make sure you're gone before I open my eyes. Why is that?"

"I've got work to do, a ranch to run. I gave Jimmy my word. I have to get an early start."

"You don't want to wake up with me because then what we have might be more than a one-night stand."

"Darlin', I'm well aware that it's not a one-night stand. It's a two-week stand and I'm a busy man."

"Then prove me wrong. Stay tonight. All night. I'll make pancakes for breakfast."

"I think I'd better leave. I've got a hundred head of cattle coming in first thing tomorrow. I need to get an early start."

"Go ahead," she called after him. "Because if you'd stayed, you just might have found out that I'm right."

SHE WAS DEAD WRONG.

Jack gunned the engine and pushed his bike faster, tearing up gravel as he headed for the ranch.

Afraid to get too close?

Like hell. He wasn't afraid. He just didn't like getting close. That way he didn't hurt anybody when the restlessness set in and he went on his way. No attachments meant no ties had to be broken. It simply made things easier for everybody.

Besides, he just plain didn't *like* getting close to people and settling in. He didn't like feeling so comfortable that he started taking each moment for granted. That's the way he'd been when his wife had passed away. Settled. Comfortable. *Happy.*

The last thought struck him and he increased his speed. Hell, he was happy now. It was just a different sort of happy. He was doing what he loved, moving from place to place, enjoying the scenery and really living his life rather than simply existing. Damn straight he was happy.

But as Jack pushed the bike harder and faster, he remembered the way he'd felt before his late wife's death. How he'd enjoyed coming home day after day, working the ranch with his dad and building his future.

Happy.

What he'd felt the past ten years didn't come close to touching that emotion. He wasn't happy now. He was simply existing.

So what? It was better than the alternative, better than risking having that happiness snatched away, like it had been so long ago. One minute he'd been young and in love. The next minute she was gone. *Gone.*

The misery had set in and nearly killed him. He'd grieved so hard, that the only way for him to cope had been to leave. To escape. To forget.

But the memories had followed him, creeping up when he least expected them. When he saw a family having dinner together at a local diner or glimpsed a man and woman grocery shopping together or simply holding hands, he thought of her. And was even worse when he knew the couple, when he knew how happy they were.

And so he ran, leaving behind the people he'd met and the friends he'd made, trading it all in for another town full of strangers. He would be all right for a little while and then the cycle would start all over and the past would catch up to him again.

Like now.

Paige had brought it all rushing back, because for the last few days, she'd shown him a happiness that he'd only dreamt of. She'd pushed past his defenses and gotten under his skin, and he liked it. Hell, he loved it. He loved her.

The realization hit him as he braked to a stop in the driveway outside the ranch house. He *did* love her.

He glanced down at the bike. He loved her, and yet instead of taking her in his arms and holding her, loving her, he was here, miles away, alone and running.

Hell, she was right. He *was* afraid to get too close. But there was one thing she'd been wrong about. He didn't fear settling down. He was settled.

That truth hit him as he walked inside the house and down the familiar hallway to the room he'd had for as long as he could remember. It was his own space, filled with his things— from his bed to his sports trophies lining the wall, his first saddle draped over a chair in the far corner to the first blue ribbon he'd won for showmanship at the Austin County Horse Show. This was his place, filled with his past, his roots.

He thought of Cecil McGraw over at the grocery, Wayne and Nell, and a dozen other people in town. His town. He'd grown up here. He always came back here. He didn't need to settle somewhere and plant roots because his roots were right here in Inspiration. His past, who he was, what he wanted, it was all in this small Texas town with his family and his friends and his woman.

His thoughts went to Paige, to the fear and desperation he'd seen in her eyes. She'd been terrified tonight, defensive, scared, and she'd pushed him away.

Jack had gladly let her because he, too, had been fearful and desperate. But no more. He'd faced his fear and conquered it. Hopefully she could do the same because Jack didn't intend to let her push him away ever again.

He walked over to his suitcase and started pulling his things out. In several minutes, he'd filled his drawers and closet and unpacked every item of clothing. With the chore came a freedom even more profound than what he felt when he was on his motorcycle, hauling ass down an empty stretch of highway.

He felt free of his past, of his fear, and now he could look to the future.

He wanted Paige Cassidy. Now and forever.

The trouble was, she didn't want him back.

Yet.

"AND SO I TOLD HIM, 'Norm, I will not wear the yellow dress. It may be your mother's favorite, but the woman hates me and I look awful in yellow.'"

"Atta girl."

"You go, Dorothy."

"Tell it like it is."

"I mean, if the woman had been the least bit nice to me, I'd wear salmon or even chartreuse, but she's constantly talking about my chicken and dumplings."

"The heathen!"

"The witch!"

"And my apple strudel."

"She's a communist, that's what she is."

"A demon straight from hell."

"And my lemon chiffon mousse..."

Paige tried to concentrate on the rest of the session. She truly did, but every time she tuned in to what was being said, something reminded her of Jack and last night and the all-important fact that she'd crossed the line. She'd pushed him away. And he probably hated her.

So? There are only three days before Jimmy and Deb get back. Then he's gone anyway. What difference does it make?

None. That's what she tried to tell herself. Three days was nothing. She'd learned so much over the past week and a half that a few days hardly mattered.

She tried to remember that, to believe it, but as the session came to a close and Paige said goodbye to the women who milled around the refreshment table, she still couldn't convince herself.

Three days was three days. Nearly half a week. A lifetime to a woman who knew next to nothing when it came to pleasing a man. What if Jack had yet to teach her some technique crucial to the whole seduction experience? She couldn't afford to miss out on even a moment, much less three entire nights.

That's what she wanted to think, rather than face the possibility that she *wanted* the next three nights with him, that she'd come to look forward to them, to *him*, and the last thing she wanted was to drive him away. She feared it had nothing to do with beefing up her education and everything to do with the fact that she liked Jack Mission.

He was handsome and sexy and nice. He listened to what she had to say and shared his own past with her. They had so much in common.

But at the same time, they were worlds apart.

The hair on the back of her neck stood on end and a strange awareness skittered over her skin. She turned.

Make that twenty or so feet apart.

He stood just inside the doorway, a grin on his face as he tipped his hat to the last SAT member who filtered out, a plate of goodies in hand. Before Paige could take her next breath, he pushed the door closed and twisted the lock. She was trapped.

Trapped?

She was being silly, yet that's how she felt as he closed in on her. Like an animal stalking its prey.

"You're not mad at me, are you? I shouldn't have said those things. It wasn't my place."

"You had every right. I called you out. Fair is fair."

"But what you fear and what you don't fear is your own business."

Jack stopped just inches shy of her, his body blocking out any means of escape. "And what do you fear, Paige?"

"Let's not start this again."

"We never finished it. You were right about me. I was afraid of getting close."

Was as in the past. Meaning he wasn't afraid now.

"That's right," he said as if he read her thoughts. "I'm not afraid anymore to get close. To get very close." He leaned down and touched her chin, tipped it so that his mouth was only inches away. "You were right and I admit it.

Now I want to hear you come clean with me. I don't want any secrets between us this time. Nothing but the two of us touching, tasting, feeling each other."

This time.

She became acutely aware of his close proximity, the hungry look in his eyes and the fact that they were all alone in broad daylight with the door locked from the inside.

"I want to see you." He reached for the top button of her blouse, the fluorescent lights blazing overhead. "Now."

"Now? But it's the middle of the day...."

"Now." He slid the first button free and moved on to the next until the shirt parted.

"I don't think—" The words caught in her throat as he touched one nipple through the lace of her bra. Before the sensation had dissipated, he unhooked her bra and freed her breasts.

Panic zipped through her and she took a deep breath. *Calm down. It's not as if you're entirely naked. You've still got your shirt, even if it isn't buttoned, and your skirt still covers the widest parts.*

A *zippp* echoed through the room and the skirt fell to her ankles. Her slip followed until she stood wearing nothing but her panties.

elbows, desperately holding the material together with her bent arms. "Please. I don't want you to see me."

"Is that what you're afraid of? That I'll see you?"

"That you won't like what you see. That you'll be turned off. That you'll turn away."

"Ah, baby," he said, cupping her face in his hands, his thumbs tracing her cheekbones. "I could never turn away from you. *Never*."

The word, filled with such sincerity, sent a warmth rushing through her body. At the same, time, a niggling doubt hit her. Something was wrong. Jack wasn't the type to say such things. He was a wanderer, a man who didn't know the meaning of never turning away.

She wanted to ask him about it, but then he pushed her back, leaned over her and blotted out the bright fluorescent lights with his hard, powerful body. Her panic eased and she gave in to the insistent throb of her nipples, eager for more of what he promised with his rasping touch.

He parted her legs, his hands sliding over the soft skin of her thighs. Sliding his hands under her buttocks, he drew her to him until her bottom lay at the edge of the table. He spread her legs wider and then he touched the heat between her legs, his fingers probing, sliding into the drenched flesh in a dizzying friction that took her breath away.

Suddenly, need took precedence over a lifetime of insecurity and she let go of the edges of her shirt. It slid free and she reached for him, pulling him close.

A quick tug at his zipper, a slide of a button and he sprang into her hands. A frantic moment later, he plunged deep, deep inside, filling her, completing her.

Her back met the table as she lay back down, her legs locked around his waist. She waited to feel him embrace her and start to move inside her, but it didn't happen.

Her eyelids fluttered open to find him staring down at her as intently as if he could see straight through her. She was completely exposed to him, vulnerable, afraid. His gaze swept the length of her, leaving nothing untouched by his visual caress. Finally, his gaze met hers and he whispered the phrase that erased years of hurt and filled her with a joy unlike anything she'd ever felt before.

"You're perfect."

But more than hearing the words, Paige actually believed them. With Jack Mission staring at her so intently, filling her so fully, she truly felt perfect.

A fleeting feeling, she knew. Jack was leaving in a few days, moving on to the next town, the next woman.

Thankfully.

Jack was dangerous to her peace of mind. He made her want more than the moment. But she could never have more with a man like Jack. She wouldn't risk it.

More was out of the question, but this…ah, *this* she could allow herself. For a little while, anyway.

10

"WHAT DO YOU MEAN you're not leaving?" Paige stood in the kitchen of the Mission Ranch three days later and tried to absorb the news Jack had just given her.

"I'm not leaving," he repeated. He leaned against the sink, a cup of coffee in his hands, a pleased expression on his face. "As in I'm staying."

"I know what not leaving means." She just didn't quite understand what it meant in regards to Jack. "But Deb and Jimmy are coming back this afternoon. This is supposed to be your last day." She held up the farewell cake she'd baked for him last night. "I even made a double fudge to honor the occasion."

And to ease the ache that had plagued her since she'd spent her very last night in Jack Mission's arms. An overwhelming feeling of loss had settled in the pit of her stomach and stayed with her, throughout a morning spent at the newspaper office and the drive all the way out to the ranch.

She hadn't expected to feel so empty at the thought of him leaving, so sad. But she did.

She had.

He wasn't leaving.

"You're *staying?*" she repeated, still trying to digest the news. "But you're not supposed to stay. You've got a job waiting for you in Santa Fe."

"I've already put in a call to this trainer I know. He's a floater like me." A determined light lit his eyes. "Like I used to be. He'll be glad to take the position until something more permanent comes up."

She shook her head and tried to quell the rush of joy that went through her at the prospect of having Jack Mission stay in Inspiration. "I don't understand. I thought you didn't want to settle down."

"I'm already settled, darlin'. Right here. This is my home. This is where my roots are. And this is where I'm staying."

"But..." *Why?* was on the tip of her tongue,

but the only thing that stumbled past her lips was a confused, "You can't." Despite the joy, she felt a rush of apprehension and fear.

Because as much as she didn't want to believe it, Paige knew that deep, down inside, she was falling for Jack Mission.

Falling, but not fallen. Not yet.

Not ever, she promised herself. Not for a man like Jack. He was a love-'em-and-leave-'em type of guy. Temporary.

And he was *staying*.

It didn't matter. His location didn't change who he was deep inside. He wasn't the forever sort. He was like Woodrow—handsome and sexy and Paige wouldn't let herself fall for such a man again.

"You can't," she repeated. Her only salvation when she'd admitted her feelings to herself that morning had been the fact that Jack was leaving. Out of sight, out of mind. That's what she'd told herself, but now... "You just can't."

"I can," he said coming up to her. He reached past her and fingered the chocolate fudge frosting on the cake she'd baked. Dipping the chocolate in his mouth, he sucked his finger. "This is good."

"Thanks. I still don't see why you changed your—"

"Want to try some?" He reached for another dollop.

"You're changing the subject."

"I'm not changing anything. The subject is closed. I'm staying right here."

She forced her heart to calm down long enough for her to draw air into her lungs. Okay, he was staying. So what? Sure, she was liable to glimpse him around town every now and then, but she could handle it. She was strong. She was in control. And she hadn't completely fallen for Jack Mission.

If he wanted to stay, it was his business because their arrangement was over. A done deal.

She ignored the sudden ache that gripped her as she watched him suckle the second dollop of chocolate from his fingertip and reached into her purse for the envelope she'd picked up at the bank.

"What's this?"

"The last order of business. Jimmy and Deb get back this afternoon, so our lessons are over."

"Darlin', we need to—"

"I appreciate everything. Thanks." She placed the envelope next to the cake and then she did the only thing she could do, with Jack standing there looking so handsome and sexy and irresistible with a speck of chocolate at the corner of his mouth and a hungry light in his eyes. Paige turned and ran for her life.

Staying or not, Jack Mission still wasn't the type of man Paige needed, a man who made her feel safe, secure, comfortable. A man who didn't have a history of running at the first sign of trouble.

A man the complete opposite of her ex-husband.

While Jack was different from Woodrow in many ways, he was also too much like him for Paige's peace of mind. She couldn't, wouldn't spend the rest of her life worrying and wondering if Jack would wake up one day and decide that she truly wasn't woman enough for him.

Not that Jack had mentioned anything about a continuing relationship. He hadn't said a word about commitment. He'd simply relayed his news.

He was *staying*.

The knowledge stayed with her and haunted her the rest of the afternoon as she tried to forget Jack Mission and get on with the rest of her life. The sad thing was, when Paige tried to picture tomorrow, all she could see was Jack's face.

Ugh, forget falling. She'd *fallen*, hook, line and sinker.

Not that it made a difference.

Jack Mission wasn't now, nor would he ever be the man for her.

"SAY THAT AGAIN," Jimmy told his brother that evening as he sat in the dining room at the Mission Ranch and loaded his plate with Nell's fried chicken. He and Deb had arrived less than an hour ago, suntanned and smiling and looking so happy that Jack felt a pang of envy.

It was crazy how things had changed. Less than two weeks ago, the sight would have sent him running. Now he couldn't help but want the same.

"I said I'm staying on here at the ranch. Since you and Deb are living at the cabin and mom's off with Redd on the senior rodeo tour, the place could use a live-in Mission to look after things."

"For how long?" Deb asked from the other side of the table.

"Permanently."

The word hung in the air for several long seconds before Jimmy finally shook his head and laughed. "If I didn't know better, I'd say I just heard the word 'permanent' come out of your mouth."

"That's what I said."

Confusion knitted Jimmy's brow. "You're kidding, right? Playing a practical joke?"

"It's no joke. I'm staying on here. I'll take care of all the horses—everything from the breeding to the breaking—and Wayne will stay on as foreman to oversee the cattle. I'd like to get into breeding horses on a commercial basis. Molly's an awful pretty filly and she'll make some fine colts."

"You are serious."

"I said I was serious."

Jimmy's fork clattered to the table as he narrowed his eyes and stared at his little brother. "What the hell happened to you while we were gone?"

"Honey, I think the question is *who* the hell happened to you while we were gone?" Deb turned a knowing smile on Jack. "What's her name?"

"Paige." The name wiped the expression from Deb's face. Her eyes widened.

"My Paige?"

"Actually, she's *my* Paige," he said with all the confidence of a man completely and totally in love. "Or she will be."

"Does that mean you have or haven't told her how you feel and she has or hasn't been accepting?"

"Well, I was going to tell her, but—"

"You *have* to tell her," Deb told him. "You have to tell her now."

But Jack intended to go one better. As stubborn as Paige was, he knew he would have to do more than simply say the words. He would have to show her, to prove to her that he didn't want to own her or control her or take charge of her life. He wanted her to make her own decisions, to be her own person.

The person he loved.

Now and forever.

"IT'S GOOD TO BE BACK."

Paige glanced up as Deb walked by carrying

the latest in her designer bitch mugs which she'd picked up on her honeymoon. She took a long sip of her steaming black coffee, leaving bright red lipstick prints on the pink ceramic mug with Bitchiest Bride in Aruba printed in neon pink letters on the outside.

"I missed this place."

"We missed you," Dolores said. "Wally almost killed us."

"It wasn't me," Wally said as he walked by, still bundled in a sweater, a ball of tissue in one hand. "It was that damned air conditioner."

"The electrician said you broke the thermostat," Deb told him.

"I did no such thing. I was trying to survive."

"Try surviving downstairs with the printing press. It's acting up again."

"You're a slave driver, you know that?"

Deb grinned and handed him a cough drop. "And proud of it." She caught Wally before he headed downstairs. "See the doc just as soon as you finish."

"I don't need to see a doctor," he said in typical man fashion. "I'll be fine. I'll—"

"See the doctor and that's an order. And then go home and go straight to bed. Alone," she added, eyeing the pile of candy bars sitting on the edge of his desk, courtesy of Paige's latest Fun Fact…*Sneak Up on Him with a Snickers.*

Hey, it wasn't Elizabeth Barrett Browning, but Paige was still new to the whole Fun Fact business.

"I'm not going home to bed. I've got an article due—"

"I'll finish it up and you *will* go home to bed, or I'll stick bamboo shoots underneath your fingernails and force feed you every one of those candy bars." She looked at Paige. "So I'm a slave driver with a heart," Deb said after Wally muttered a grudging "Okay," and disappeared down the stairs. "Besides," she told Paige who stared knowingly at her, "I can't very well have him here infecting my entire staff. It's purely a business decision."

"Sure." Deb was what Wally termed an "Eskimo Pie." She liked to talk tough on the outside, but inside she was soft and nice and she'd been Paige's first friend at a time when she'd really needed one. She still was.

"So," Deb said once she'd settled at her desk and taken another sip of her coffee. "I hear you and Jack got a little friendly while we were gone."

"We, um, did spend some time together." Her brain searched for a plausible explanation as she wondered exactly how much Deb knew. Had Jack told her?

No, he wouldn't do that. He wasn't a man to kiss and tell, and he certainly wouldn't confess all to his new sister-in-law. He and Deb hardly knew each other.

Then again, the woman had ways...

Paige contemplated the notion for several seconds before completely dismissing it. Ways or not, Jack wasn't a man to be cornered into telling anything by anyone. Deb had probably heard rumors about them being seen around town, Paige figured after a few silent seconds when Deb didn't press the issue. Deb wasn't one to beat around the bush. She was a straight shooter and if she had known the extent of their relationship, she would have come out and ask for a progress report, or at least shouted some encouragement.

"He was, um, helping me with one of my classes," Paige continued, salving her conscious over lying to her friend.

"Which one?"

"A new one. I just started. Say, I've really got to get going. I'm covering the ladies' auxiliary luncheon in a half hour."

"That's Dolores's job."

"She's at the hair salon. Ida Joe found out that her husband was sleeping with his secretary over at the construction site. But that's not all. It seems his secretary is doing one better and sleeping with her other boss, who slept with Ida Joe's niece last year at the Christmas party."

"Sounds complicated."

"It is. They're having an emergency perm and color session over at the Cut-n-Curl to discuss everything and see if they've left anyone out of the sleeping circle."

"So are you going to see Jack again?" Deb asked a split second before Paige walked out the door.

"I don't think—"

"Yes." Jack's deep voice cut into her thoughts and she turned to find him standing in the doorway barely a few inches from her. He wore black jeans, a motorcycle T-shirt and a leather vest. He looked the typical free spirit that he was.

That he used to be.

He was *staying*.

"I—I'm busy," she blurted, fear and panic whirling into a dangerous mix. "I'm on my way to the recreation center."

"I'll drive you."

Before she could protest, he took her hand, his fingers twining with hers, and led her out the door.

"THIS ISN'T the recreation center." Paige stared at the boarded-up building that sat in the middle of downtown just a few blocks from city hall. It used to be an insurance agency that had been converted into a bed and breakfast a few years back. Had eventually gone out of business when the Wallabys had renovated their ranch house as a resort. Gray paint curled and peeled in several spots. Boards blocked most of the windows.

But it wasn't the decaying building that caught her eye. It was the shiny new sign hanging from a chain on the front porch. *Paige's House.*

She shook her head. "I don't understand."

"This is your new meeting spot."

"What are you talking about?"

"For your SAT group."

"You're saying this building is ours?"

"For the next five years." He handed her some folded documents. "This is a five-year lease. You can move in anytime. We should fix the place up first, though. Maybe give it a coat of paint and a good cleaning and—"

"But how? When? *Why?*" The questions raced through her mind, stirring her heartbeat and making her blood pound. She didn't understand any of this.

"I couldn't take your money," he told her.

"Are you saying you bought this with the hundred dollars I gave you?"

"Actually, your money bought that sign. The place is courtesy of Walter Turnover."

"Jenny's husband?"

"I talked to him and convinced him that the one thing this town needed was a women's shelter. Someplace where they could go and get counseling. Where he and his wife could seek counseling if they wanted to."

The meaning of his words sank in and warmth spread through her, along with dread. "You talked to him about Jenny? You didn't tell him she's been coming to the meetings."

"I just mentioned that she looked unhappy and that if he loved her, he would find out why. This seemed like the place to do it."

"You shouldn't have—"

"I know when to interfere and when not to. Walter isn't a bad man. You said yourself that Jenny looks beaten down emotionally, not physically."

"It's still a chance you shouldn't have taken."

"I wouldn't have taken it if there had been any risk. I've known Walter my entire life. And Jenny. And I talked with the sheriff to make sure there'd been no reports of any type of abuse or violence. Then I sat down with him, man to man. He's hardheaded and domineering, but he does love his wife. I don't think he even realized how his behavior had been affecting her until I mentioned to him that she didn't look as happy as the last time I'd seen her. That made him think." He took her hand. "That's the 'how.' The 'when' was yesterday. And the 'why' is because—"

"Don't." She shook her head, panic rushing through her and making her heart pump all the faster. "Please don't say it."

"I love you, Paige. I wanted to show you how much and I couldn't think of a better way to do it than to give you what you've been wanting more than anything in the world, to show you that your dreams and your hopes are important to me. That you're important to me."

"I..." She fought back a wave of tears. "I appreciate it, but..." This wasn't fair. She didn't want him to love her. He wasn't the man for her. He wasn't her type.

"Tell me you love me."

The realization hit her as she sat there next to him, the shelter she'd dreamt of so many times right in front of her eye, thanks to Jack. She *did* love him.

She'd always loved him, from the first moment she'd spotted him through her video lens.

Joy rushed through her, followed by an all-consuming dread that sent her scrambling from the truck and running for her life. Because Paige Cassidy had done the one thing she'd vowed never to do again. She'd fallen for the wrong man and made the same mistake all over again.

But she didn't have to walk the same path. She might love Jack, but she didn't have to admit to that love. She didn't have to commit herself to him and wind up back in the very same situation as before, with the same type of man. Even if that man was Jack Mission.

No matter how much she suddenly wanted to.

11

Jack Mission was totally different from her sorry, low-down, snake-in-the-grass ex-husband.

Paige came to that conclusion over the next few weeks as she kept her distance and tried to forget all about Jack, the way he touched her, kissed her, smiled at her and said "I love you."

She tried to forget, but she couldn't. The words haunted her as much as the man himself. She thought she'd catch the occasional glimpse of him around town when she'd first heard he was staying. Instead she saw him every day. Several times a day. He showed up at her office to walk her to this interview or that story. He brought her lunch. He showed up at her house in the evening to help water her yard. He was everywhere she looked. Worse, he was in her head. Her heart.

Because she loved him.

Not because he was so much like Woodrow

and she'd been fooled once before. She loved him because he was different. Because he made her feel different. He made her feel smart and pretty and important.

More than that, he made her believe all those things about herself. She *was* smart and pretty and important, and worthy of a man's love. Of Jack's love.

He wasn't Woodrow. Woodrow had been a taker. He'd taken her love and sense of self and everything until she'd had nothing left inside. But Jack was a giver.

He'd given her back everything she'd lost and more. His love, his admiration, his praise, his sincerity, his heart...

Yes, he'd given her his heart and she'd yet to figure out what she was going to do with it.

"Dump 'im!" The shout came from Sue Groff, who shouted encouragement to Delilah Sue Wilkins, who was currently bashing the boyfriend who'd bought her a toaster for their one-month anniversary.

Paige forced her thoughts from Jack to the first SAT meeting in their brand-new location. *Paige's House*.

"I say if the man can't be more in tune with what a woman likes, then who needs him?"

"Are you kidding?" someone asked. "They can't be in tune when they're all a bunch of idiots. The whole lot of 'em."

"And babies," someone else added. "Not a one of 'em could withstand even one labor pain."

"They're self-absorbed jerks," another woman said. "I swear, if I have to see any more butt patting on national television during a football game, I'm liable to puke."

"Men," one woman declared. "Who needs 'em?"

Before Paige realized what she was doing, her hand slid into the air. "I do," she said.

Stunned silence held the room captive for the space of several heartbeats, before hands started sliding into the air as the rest of the women joined in, including Jenny Turnover, who'd had the first official counseling session at Paige's House just yesterday with her husband, Walter.

Paige hadn't sat in on the session, but she'd heard from Jenny herself that they'd talked more in an hour than they'd talked in the past five years. They still had a lot of work ahead of them, but Jenny was optimistic, and she was smiling again.

"I need a man. My man," Paige said, and the words didn't bring the same dread they had a few weeks before.

Because Paige wasn't afraid anymore. She trusted Jack. And she loved him. Now all she had to do was tell him.

SHE HATED HIM.

Jack finally admitted the truth to himself as he saddled Molly and prepared for her first ride. Gone was the wild animal who'd nearly stomped him to death. She was as calm as the Gulf on a hot Texas day, and just as pretty.

He'd won with her, but not with Paige.

He'd tried, but she was stubborn. Maybe too stubborn.

"I just can't get through to her, girl." He rubbed Molly's neck. "At least I've got you to talk to. You don't mind listening, do you, girl? I'm not such a bad guy. Decent looking. Sexy as hell. Don't you think?"

"I'm out of sight for five minutes, and you're already flirting with another woman."

Paige's voice drew him around and he turned to find her standing in the barn doorway. She wore an oversized baggy dress that hid her luscious shape and a smile. He didn't think he'd ever seen a woman look more beautiful.

"She's pretty," she said, crossing the distance between them and coming up next to him. "You've definitely got good taste when it comes to women."

"When it comes to one woman—you. I love you," he said again, as if that would tip the scales in his favor. If only it would.

"I've been giving that a lot of thought and I've come to the conclusion that you're going to have to stop stalking me."

"Stalking you?"

"Yeah. You show up everywhere, uninvited. That definitely qualifies as stalking. It has to stop."

His nostrils flared as the meaning of what she was saying sank in. She didn't want him around. She wanted him to leave her alone. "So what are you trying to say?"

Leave me alone. The words stood unspoken between them as they stared at each other. And then she smiled and his heart started beating again.

"That this uninvited business has to stop."

"Meaning?"

"Meaning, I'm giving you an invitation."

"To stalk you?"

"To love me." Her smile disappeared as a serious light lit her eyes. "Because I love you. I was scared. I'm still scared. But you're worth the risk. What we have is worth the risk."

Joy rushed through him and he hauled her into his arms, holding her close as if he never meant to let her go.

Because he didn't. Not now. Not ever.

"Marry me," he said, pulling back to look at her. "Marry me and have my kids and give me forever."

She tilted her head back and smiled up at him. He saw his future right there in her eyes. "I thought you'd never ask."

It's hot...and it's out of control.

This winter is going to be *hot, hot, hot!*
Don't miss these bold, provocative,
ultra-sexy books!

SEDUCED by Janelle Denison
December 2000

Lawyer Ryan Matthews wanted sexy Jessica Newman the
moment he saw her. And she seemed to want him, too, but
something was holding her back. So Ryan decides it's time
to launch a sensual assault. He *is* going to have Jessica in
his bed—and he isn't above tempting her with her own
forbidden fantasies to do it....

SIMPLY SENSUAL by Carly Phillips
January 2001

When P.I. Ben Callahan agrees to take the job of watching
over spoiled heiress Grace Montgomery, he figures it's easy
money. That is, until he discovers gorgeous Grace has a
reckless streak a mile wide and is a serious threat to his
libido—and his heart. Ben isn't worried about keeping
Grace safe. But can he protect her from his loving lies?

Don't miss this daring duo!

HARLEQUIN®
Temptation.

Visit us at www.eHarlequin.com   HTBLAZEW

Tyler Brides

It happened one weekend...

Quinn and Molly Spencer are delighted to accept three
bookings for their newly opened B&B, Breakfast Inn Bed,
located in America's favorite hometown, Tyler, Wisconsin.

But Gina Santori is anything but thrilled to discover her
best friend has tricked her into sharing a room with
the man who broke her heart eight years ago....

And Delia Mayhew can hardly believe that she's
gotten herself locked in the Breakfast Inn Bed
basement with the sexiest man in America.

Then there's Rebecca Salter. She's turned up at the
Inn in her wedding gown. Minus her groom.

*Come home to Tyler for three delightful novellas
by three of your favorite authors: Kristine Rolofson,
Heather MacAllister and Jacqueline Diamond.*

HARLEQUIN®
Makes any time special ™

Visit us at www.eHarlequin.com PHTB

MURIEL JENSEN

Bride by Surprise

Three lighthearted stories of marriages that aren't quite what they seem...

If Charlotte Morreaux had gotten married, it wouldn't have been to her nemesis Derek Cabot. But fate and her stepmother contrived to force them both into a lie that snowballed uncontrollably.

When Barbara Ryan's boss, John Cheney, and a cluster of clergymen found her in his office—half-naked—he planted a kiss on her lips and introduced her as his blushing bride. And the new mother of his twin boys!

Patrick Gallagher was looking for money, not a wife. But marrying Regina Raleigh was a condition of his loan. Now on the run from a predator, they realized there was another problem confronting them—lust!

HARLEQUIN
Makes any time special

Look for BRIDE BY SURPRISE on sale in December 2000.

Visit us at www.eHarlequin.com

PBR3BBS

Pamela Burford presents

The
Wedding
Ring

*Four high school friends and a pact—
every girl gets her ideal mate by thirty or be
prepared for matchmaking! The rules are
simple. Give your "chosen" man three
months...and see what happens!*

Love's Funny That Way
Temptation #812—on sale December 2000
It's no joke when Raven Muldoon falls in love with comedy
club owner Hunter—*brother* of her "intended."

I Do, But Here's the Catch
Temptation #816—on sale January 2001
Charli Ross is more than willing to give up her status as
last of a dying breed—the thirty-year-old virgin—to Grant.
But all *he* wants is marriage.

One Eager Bride To Go
Temptation #820—on sale February 2001
Sunny Bleecker is still waiting tables at Wafflemania when
Kirk comes home from California and wants to marry her.
It's as if all her dreams have finally come true—except...

Fiancé for Hire
Temptation #824—on sale March 2001
No way is Amanda Coppersmith going to let
The Wedding Ring rope her into marriage. But no matter
how clever she is, Nick is one step ahead of her...

*"Pamela Burford creates the
memorable characters readers love!"
—The Literary Times*

Visit us at www.eHarlequin.com   HTRING

ROMANTIC FANTASIES COME ALIVE WITH

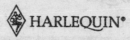

HARLEQUIN®

INTIMACIES

Harlequin is turning up the heat with
this seductive collection!

Experience the passion as the heroes and heroines explore
their deepest desires, their innermost secrets. Get lost in
these tantalizing stories that will leave you wanting more!

Available in November at your favorite retail outlet:

OUT OF CONTROL by Candace Schuler
NIGHT RHYTHMS by Elda Minger
SCANDALIZED! by Lori Foster
PRIVATE FANTASIES by Janelle Denison

Visit us at www.eHarlequin.com   PHINT1

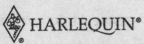

HARLEQUIN®

makes any time special—online...

eHARLEQUIN.com

your romantic escapes

—Indulgences—
♥ Monthly guides to indulging yourself,
such as:
  ★ Tub Time: A guide for bathing beauties
  ★ Magic Massages: A treat for tired feet

—Horoscopes—
♥ Find your daily Passionscope, weekly
Lovescopes and Erotiscopes
♥ Try our compatibility game

—Reel Love—
♥ Read all the latest romantic
movie reviews

—Royal Romance—
♥ Get the latest scoop on your favorite
royal romances

—Romantic Travel—
♥ For the most romantic destinations, hotels
and travel activities

HINTE1

MAITLAND MATERNITY

Where the luckiest babies are born!

Join Harlequin® and Silhouette® for a special 12-book series about the world-renowned Maitland Maternity Clinic, owned and operated by the prominent Maitland family of Austin, Texas, where romances are born, secrets are revealed...and bundles of joy are delivered!

Look for

MAITLAND MATERNITY

titles at your favorite retail outlet, starting in August 2000

HARLEQUIN®
Makes any time special ™

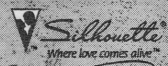

Silhouette
Where love comes alive ™

Visit us at www.eHarlequin.com   PHMMGEN

This Christmas, experience
the love, warmth and magic that
only Harlequin can provide with

*Mistletoe
Magic*

a charming collection from

BETTY NEELS

MARGARET WAY   REBECCA WINTERS

Available November 2000

HARLEQUIN®
Makes any time special™

Visit us at www.eHarlequin.com   PHMAGIC